PERRAULT'S
FAIRY TALES

Perrault's Fairy Tales

Translated by
A. E. Johnson

WORDSWORTH CLASSICS

For my husband
ANTHONY JOHN RANSON
with love from your wife, the publisher.
Eternally grateful for your unconditional love.

Readers who are interested in other titles from
Wordsworth Editions are invited to visit our website at
www.wordsworth-editions.com

For our latest list and a full mail-order service, contact
Bibliophile Books, 5 Datapoint, South Crescent, London E16 4TL
TEL: +44 (0)20 7474 2474 FAX: +44 (0)20 7474 8589
ORDERS: orders@bibliophilebooks.com
WEBSITE: www.bibliophilebooks.com

This edition published in 2004 by Wordsworth Editions Limited
8B East Street, Ware, Hertfordshire SG12 9HJ

ISBN 978 1 84022 482 5

Text © Wordsworth Editions Limited 2004

Wordsworth® is a registered trade mark of
Wordsworth Editions Limited

Wordsworth Editions
is the company founded in 1987 by
MICHAEL TRAYLER

Typeset in Great Britain by Antony Gray
Printed and bound by Clays Ltd, St Ives plc

Preface

Of the twelve tales which comprise this volume, the first eight are from the master hand of Charles Perrault. Perrault (1628–1703) enjoyed much distinction in his day and is familiar to students of French literature for the prominent part he played in the famous *Quarrel of the Ancients and Moderns*, which so keenly occupied French men of letters in the latter part of the seventeenth century. But his fame today rests upon his authorship of the traditional *Tales of Mother Goose; or Stories of Olden Times*, and so long as there are children to listen spellbound to the adventures of Cinderella, Red Riding Hood, and that arch rogue Puss in Boots, his memory will endure.

Three of the tales, 'The Ridiculous Wishes', 'Donkey-Skin' and 'Patient Griselda', are seldom included within collections of Perrault's work, because they were originally written in a very florid and diffuse verse form. They are reproduced here by paraphrase rather than by literal translation and no attempt has been made to imitate the complex rhyme and metre of the author's original work. The 'Patient Griselda' story is not a Perrault invention, having been used earlier by Boccaccio, Chaucer and others.

The last story, 'Beauty and the Beast', although not by Perrault (it was penned by Mme. Leprince de Beaumont [1711–1781]), has a similarity of style and celebrity which justifiably merits its inclusion.

With the exception of the morals and the three tales taken from verse, the translations are by A. E. Johnson.

Contents

THE STORIES

The Sleeping Beauty in the Wood

ONCE UPON A TIME there lived a king and queen who were grieved, more grieved than words can tell, because they had no children. They tried the waters of every country, made vows and pilgrimages, and did everything that could be done, but without result. At last, however, the queen found that her wishes were fulfilled, and in due course she gave birth to a daughter.

A grand christening was held, and all the fairies that could be found in the realm (they numbered seven in all) were invited to be godmothers to the little princess. This was done so that by means of the gifts which each in turn would bestow upon her (in accordance with the fairy custom of those days) the princess might be endowed with every imaginable perfection.

When the christening ceremony was over, all the company returned to the king's palace, where a great banquet was held in honour of the fairies. Places were laid for them in magnificent style, and before each was placed a solid gold casket containing a spoon, fork, and knife of fine gold, set with diamonds and rubies. But just as all were sitting down to table an aged fairy was seen to enter, whom no one had thought to invite – the reason being that for more than fifty years she had never quitted the tower in which she lived, and people had supposed her to be dead or bewitched.

By the king's orders a place was laid for her, but it was impossible to give her a golden casket like the others, for only seven had been made for the seven fairies. The old creature believed that she was intentionally slighted, and muttered threats between her teeth.

She was overheard by one of the young fairies, who was seated near by. The latter, guessing that some mischievous gift might be bestowed upon the little princess, hid behind the tapestry as soon as the company left the table. Her intention was to be the last to speak, and so to have the power of counteracting, as far as possible, any evil which the old fairy might do.

Presently the fairies began to bestow their gifts upon the princess. The youngest ordained that she should be the most beautiful person in the world; the next, that she should have the temper of an angel; the third, that she should do everything with wonderful grace; the fourth, that she should dance to perfection; the fifth, that she should sing like a nightingale; and the sixth, that she should play every kind of music with the utmost skill.

It was now the turn of the aged fairy. Shaking her

head, in token of spite rather than of infirmity, she declared that the princess should prick her hand with a spindle, and die of it. A shudder ran through the company at this terrible gift. All eyes were filled with tears.

But at this moment the young fairy stepped forth from behind the tapestry.

"Take comfort your Majesties," she cried in a loud voice; "your daughter shall not die. My power, it is true, is not enough to undo all that my aged kinswoman has decreed: the princess will indeed prick her hand with a spindle. But instead of dying she shall merely fall into a profound slumber that will last a hundred years. At the end of that time a king's son shall come to awaken her."

The king, in an attempt to avert the unhappy doom pronounced by the old fairy, at once published an edict forbidding all persons, under pain of death, to use a spinning-wheel or keep a spindle in the house.

At the end of the fifteen or sixteen years the king and queen happened one day to be away, on pleasure bent. The princess was running about the castle, and going upstairs from room to room she came at length to a garret at the top of a tower, where an old serving-woman sat alone with her distaff, spinning. This good woman had never heard speak of the king's proclamation forbidding the use of spinning-wheels.

"What are you doing, my good woman?" asked the princess.

"I am spinning, my pretty child," replied the dame,

not knowing who she was.

"Oh, what fun!" rejoined the princess; "how do you do it? Let me try and see if I can do it equally well."

Partly because she was too hasty, partly because she was a little heedless, but also because the fairy decree had ordained it, no sooner had she seized the spindle than she pricked her hand and fell down in a swoon.

In great alarm the good dame cried out for help. People came running from every quarter to the princess. They threw water on her face, chafed her with their hands, and rubbed her temples with the royal essence of Hungary. But nothing would restore her.

Then the king, who had been brought upstairs by the commotion, remembered the fairy prophecy. Feeling certain that what had happened was inevitable, since the fairies had decreed it, he gave orders that the princess should be placed in the finest apartment in the palace, upon a bed embroidered in gold and silver.

You would have thought her an angel, so fair was she to behold. The trance had not taken away the lovely colour of her complexion. Her cheeks were delicately flushed, her lips like coral. Her eyes, indeed, were closed, but her gentle breathing could be heard, and it was therefore plain that she was not dead. The king commanded that she should be left to sleep in peace until the hour of her awakening should come.

When the accident happened to the princess, the good fairy who had saved her life by condemning her to sleep a hundred years was in the kingdom of Mataquin, twelve thousand leagues away. She was instantly warned of it, however, by a little dwarf who had a pair of seven-league boots, which are boots that enable one to cover seven leagues at a single step. The fairy set off at once, and within an hour her chariot of fire, drawn by dragons, was seen approaching.

The king handed her down from her chariot, and she approved of all that he had done. But being gifted with great powers of foresight, she bethought herself that when the princess came to be awakened, she would be much distressed to find herself all alone in the old castle. And this is what she did.

She touched with her wand everybody (except the king and queen) who was in the castle – governesses, maids of honour, ladies-in-waiting, gentlemen, officers, stewards, cooks, scullions, errand boys, guards, porters, pages, footmen. She touched likewise all the horses in the stables, with their grooms, the big mastiffs in the courtyard, and little Puff, the pet dog of the princess, who was lying on the bed beside his mistress. The moment she had touched them they all fell asleep, to awaken only at the same moment as their mistress. Thus they would always be ready with their service whenever she should require it. The very spits before the fire, loaded with partridges and pheasants, subsided into slumber, and the fire as well. All was done in a moment, for the fairies do not take long over their work.

Then the king and queen kissed their dear child, without waking her, and left the castle. Proclamations were issued, forbidding any approach to it, but these warnings were not needed, for within a quarter of an hour there grew up all round the park so vast a quantity of trees big and small, with interlacing brambles and thorns, that neither man nor beast could penetrate them. The tops alone of the castle towers could be seen, and these only from a distance. Thus did the fairy's magic contrive that the princess, during all the time of her slumber, should have nought whatever to fear from prying eyes.

At the end of a hundred years the throne had passed to another family from that of the sleeping princess. One day the king's son chanced to go a-hunting that way, and seeing in the distance some towers in the midst of a large and dense forest, he asked what they were. His attendants told him in reply the various stories which they had heard. Some said there was an old castle haunted by ghosts, others that all the witches of the neighbourhood held their revels there. The favourite tale was that in the castle lived an ogre, who carried thither all the children whom he could catch. There he devoured them at his leisure, and since he was the only person who could force a passage through the wood nobody had been able to pursue him.

While the prince was wondering what to believe, an old peasant took up the tale.

"Your Highness," said he, "more than fifty years ago I heard my father say that in this castle lies a princess, the most beautiful that has ever been seen. It is her doom to sleep there for a hundred years, and then to be awakened by a king's son, for whose coming she waits."

This story fired the young prince. He jumped immediately to the conclusion that it was for him to see so gay an adventure through, and impelled alike by the wish for love and glory, he resolved to set about it on the spot.

Hardly had he taken a step towards the wood when the tall trees, the brambles and the thorns, separated of themselves and made a path for him. He turned in the direction of the castle, and espied it at the end of a long avenue. This avenue he entered, and was surprised to notice that the trees closed up again as soon as he had passed, so that none of his retinue was able to follow him. A young and gallant prince is always brave, however; so he continued on his way, and presently reached a large fore-court.

The sight that now met his gaze was enough to fill him with an icy fear. The silence of the place was dreadful, and death seemed all about him. The recumbent figures of men and animals had all the appearance of being lifeless, until he perceived by the pimply noses and ruddy faces of the porters that they merely slept. It was plain, too, from their glasses, in which were still some dregs of wine, that they had fallen asleep while drinking.

The prince made his way into a great courtyard, paved with marble, and mounting the staircase entered the guard- room. Here the guards were lined up on either side in two ranks, their muskets on their shoulders, snoring their hardest. Through several apartments crowded with ladies and gentlemen-in-waiting, some seated, some standing, but all asleep, he pushed on, and so came at last to a chamber which was decked all over with gold. There he encountered the most beautiful sight he had ever seen. Reclining upon a bed, the curtains of which on every side were drawn back, was a princess of seemingly some fifteen or sixteen summers, whose radiant beauty had an almost unearthly lustre.

Trembling in his admiration he drew near and went on his knees beside her. At the same moment, the hour of disenchantment having come, the princess awoke, and bestowed upon him a look more tender than a first glance might seem to warrant.

"Is it you, dear prince?" she said; "you have been long in coming!"

Charmed by these words, and especially by the manner in which they were said, the prince scarcely knew how to express his delight and gratification. He declared that he loved her better than he loved himself. His words were faltering, but they pleased the more for that. The less there is of eloquence, the more there is of love.

Her embarrassment was less than his, and that is not to be wondered at, since she had had time to think of what she would say to him. It seems (although the story says nothing about it) that the good fairy had beguiled her long slumber with pleasant dreams. To be brief, after four hours of talking they had not succeeded in uttering one half of the things they had to say to each other.

Now the whole palace had awakened with the princess. Every one went about his business, and since they were not all in love they presently began to feel mortally hungry. The lady-in-waiting, who was suffering like the rest, at length lost patience, and in a loud voice called out to the princess that supper was served.

The princess was already fully dressed, and in most magnificent style. As he helped her to rise, the prince refrained from telling her that her clothes, with the straight collar which she wore, were like those to which his grandmother had been accustomed. And in truth, they in no way detracted from her beauty.

They passed into an apartment hung with mirrors, and were there served with supper by the stewards of the household, while the fiddles and oboes played some old music – and played it remarkably well, considering they had not played at all for just upon a hundred years. A little later, when supper was over, the chaplain married them in the castle chapel, and in due course, attended by the courtiers in waiting, they retired to rest.

They slept but little, however. The princess, indeed, had not much need of sleep, and as soon as morning came the prince took his leave of her. He returned to the city, and told his father, who was awaiting him with some anxiety, that he had lost himself while hunting in the forest, but had obtained some black bread and cheese from a charcoal-burner, in whose hovel he had passed the night. His royal father, being of an easy-going nature, believed the tale, but his mother was not so easily hoodwinked. She noticed that he now went hunting every day, and that he always had an excuse handy when he had slept two or three nights from home. She felt certain, therefore, that he had some love affair.

Two whole years passed since the marriage of the prince and princess, and during that time they had two children. The first, a daughter, was called "Dawn," while the second, a boy, was named "Day," because he seemed even more beautiful than his sister.

Many a time the queen told her son that he ought to settle down in life. She tried in this way to make him confide in her, but he did not dare to trust her with his secret. Despite the affection which he bore her, he was afraid of his mother, for she came of a race of ogres, and the king had only married her for her wealth.

It was whispered at the Court that she had ogrish instincts, and that when little children were near her she had the greatest difficulty in the world to keep herself from pouncing on them.

No wonder the prince was reluctant to say a word.

But at the end of two years the king died, and the prince found himself on the throne. He then made public announcement of his marriage, and went in state to fetch his royal consort from her castle. With her two children beside her she made a triumphal entry into the capital of her husband's realm.

Some time afterwards the king declared war on his

neighbour, the Emperor Cantalabutte. He appointed the queen-mother as regent in his absence, and entrusted his wife and children to her care.

He expected to be away at the war for the whole of the summer, and as soon as he was gone the queen-mother sent her daughter-in-law and the two children to a country mansion in the forest. This she did that she might be able the more easily to gratify her horrible longings. A few days later she went there herself, and in the evening summoned the chief steward.

"For my dinner to-morrow," she told him, "I will eat little Dawn."

"Oh, Madam!" exclaimed the steward.

"That is my will," said the queen; and she spoke in the tones of an ogre who longs for raw meat.

"You will serve her with piquant sauce," she added.

The poor man, seeing plainly that it was useless to trifle with an ogress, took his big knife and went up to little Dawn's chamber. She was at that time four years old, and when she came running with a smile to greet him, flinging her arms round his neck and coaxing him to give her some sweets, he burst into tears, and let the knife fall from his hand.

Presently he went down to the yard behind the house, and slaughtered a young lamb. For this he made so delicious a sauce that his mistress declared she had never eaten anything so good.

At the same time the steward carried little Dawn to his wife, and bade the latter hide her in the quarters which they had below the yard.

Eight days later the wicked queen summoned her steward again.

"For my supper," she announced, "I will eat little Day."

The steward made no answer, being determined to trick her as he had done previously. He went in search of little Day, whom he found with a tiny foil in his hand, making brave passes – though he was but three years old – at a big monkey. He carried him off to his wife, who stowed him away in hiding with little Dawn. To the ogress the steward served up, in place of Day, a young kid so tender that she found it surprisingly delicious.

So far, so good. But there came an evening when this evil queen again addressed the steward.

"I have a mind," she said, "to eat the queen with the same sauce as you served with her children."

This time the poor steward despaired of being able to practice another deception. The young queen was twenty years old, without counting the hundred years she had been asleep. Her skin, though white and beautiful, had become a little tough, and what animal could he possibly find that would correspond to her? He made up his mind that if he would save his own life he must kill the queen, and went upstairs to her apartment determined to do the deed once and for all. Goading himself into a rage he drew his knife and entered the young queen's chamber, but a reluctance to give her no moment of grace made him repeat respectfully the command which he had received from the queen-mother.

"Do it! do it!" she cried, baring her neck to him; "carry out the order you have been given! Then once more I shall see my children, my poor children that I loved so much!"

Nothing had been said to her when the children were stolen away, and she believed them to be dead.

The poor steward was overcome by compassion. "No, no, Madam," he declared; "you shall not die, but you shall certainly see your children again. That will be in my quarters, where I have hidden them. I shall make the queen eat a young hind in place of you, and thus trick her once more."

Without more ado he led her to his quarters, and leaving her there to embrace and weep over her children, proceeded to cook a hind with such art that the queen-mother ate it for her supper with as much appetite as if it had indeed been the young queen.

The queen-mother felt well satisfied with her cruel deeds, and planned to tell the king, on his return, that savage wolves had devoured his consort and his children. It was her habit, however, to prowl often about the courts and alleys of the mansion, in the hope of scenting raw meat, and one evening she heard the little boy Day crying in a basement cellar. The child was weeping because his mother had threatened to whip him for some naughtiness, and she heard at the same time the voice of Dawn begging forgiveness for her brother.

The ogress recognised the voices of the queen and her children, and was enraged to find she had been tricked. The next morning, in tones so affrighting that all trembled, she ordered a huge vat to be brought into the middle of the courtyard. This she filled with vipers and toads, with snakes and serpents of every kind, intending to cast into it the queen and her children, and the steward and his wife and serving-girl. By her command these were brought forward, with their hands tied behind their backs.

There they were, and her minions were making ready to cast them into the vat, when into the courtyard rode the king! Nobody had expected him so soon, but he had travelled post-haste. Filled with amazement, he demanded to know what this horrible spectacle meant. None dared tell him, and at that moment the ogress, enraged at what confronted her, threw herself head foremost into the vat, and was devoured on the instant by the hideous creatures she had placed in it.

The king could not but be sorry, for after all she was his mother; but it was not long before he found ample consolation in his beautiful wife and children.

MORAL

To wait a bit in choosing a husband
Rich, courteous, genteel and kind;
That is understandable enough.

But to wait a hundred years, and all the time asleep,
Not many maidens would be found with
such patience.
This story, however, seems to prove
That marriage bonds,
Even though they be delayed, are none the
less blissful,
And that one loses nothing by waiting.
But maidens yearn for the wedding joys
With so much ardour
That I have neither strength nor the heart
To preach this moral to them.

Puss in Boots

**A** CERTAIN MILLER had three sons, and when he died the sole worldly goods which he bequeathed to them were his mill, his ass, and his cat. This little legacy was very quickly divided up, and you may be quite sure that neither notary nor attorney were called in to help, for they would speedily have grabbed it all for themselves.

The eldest son took the mill, and the second son took the ass. Consequently all that remained for the youngest son was the cat, and he was not a little disappointed at receiving such a miserable portion.

"My brothers," said he, "will be able to get a decent living by joining forces, but for my part, as soon as I have eaten my cat and made a muff out of his skin, I am bound to die of hunger."

These remarks were overheard by Puss, who pretended not to have been listening, and said very soberly and seriously:

"There is not the least need for you to worry, Master. All you have to do is to give me a pouch, and get me a pair of boots made for me so that I can walk in the woods. You will find then that your share is not so bad after all."

Now this cat had often shown himself capable of performing cunning tricks. When catching rats and mice, for example, he would hide himself amongst the meal and hang downwards by the feet as though he were dead. His master, therefore, though he did not build too much on what the cat had said, felt some hope of being assisted in his miserable plight.

On receiving the boots which he had asked for, Puss gaily pulled them on. Then he hung the pouch round his neck, and holding the cords which tied it in front of him with his paws, he sallied forth to a warren where rabbits abounded. Placing some bran and lettuce in the pouch, he stretched himself out and lay as if dead. His plan was to wait until some young rabbit, unlearned in worldly wisdom, should come and rummage in the pouch for the eatables which he had placed there.

Hardly had he laid himself down when things fell out as he wished. A stupid young rabbit went into the pouch, and Master Puss, pulling the cords tight, killed him on the instant.

Well satisfied with his capture, Puss departed to the king's palace. There he demanded an audience, and was ushered upstairs. He entered the royal apartment, and bowed profoundly to the king.

"I bring you, Sire," said he, "a rabbit from the warren of the marquis of Carabas (such was the title he invented for his master), which I am bidden to present to you on his behalf."

"Tell your master," replied the king, "that I thank him, and am pleased by his attention."

Another time the cat hid himself in a wheatfield, keeping the mouth of his bag wide open. Two partridges ventured in, and by pulling the cords tight he captured both of them. Off he went and presented them to the king, just as he had done with the rabbit from the warren. His Majesty was not less gratified by the brace of partridges, and handed the cat a present for himself.

For two or three months Puss went on in this way, every now and again taking to the king, as a present from his master, some game which he had caught. There came a day when he learned that the king intended to take his daughter, who was the most beautiful princess in the world, for an excursion along the river bank.

"If you will do as I tell you," said Puss to his master, "your fortune is made. You have only to go and bathe in the river at the spot which I shall point out to you. Leave the rest to me."

The marquis of Carabas had no idea what plan was afoot, but did as the cat had directed.

While he was bathing the king drew near, and Puss at once began to cry out at the top of his voice:

"Help! help! the marquis of Carabas is drowning!"

At these shouts the king put his head out of the carriage window. He recognised the cat who had so often brought him game, and bade his escort go speedily to the help of the marquis of Carabas.

While they were pulling the poor marquis out of the

river, Puss approached the carriage and explained to the king that while his master was bathing robbers had come and taken away his clothes, though he had cried "Stop, thief!" at the top of his voice. As a matter of fact, the rascal had hidden them under a big stone. The king at once commanded the keepers of his wardrobe to go and select a suit of his finest clothes for the marquis of Carabas.

The king received the marquis with many compliments, and as the fine clothes which the latter had just put on set off his good looks (for he was handsome and comely in appearance), the king's daughter found him very much to her liking. Indeed, the marquis of Carabas had not bestowed more than two or three respectful but sentimental glances upon her when she fell madly in love with him. The king invited him to enter the coach and join the party.

Delighted to see his plan so successfully launched, the cat went on ahead, and presently came upon some peasants who were mowing a field.

"Listen, my good fellows," said he; "if you do not tell the king that the field which you are mowing belongs to the marquis of Carabas, you will all be chopped up into little pieces like mincemeat."

In due course the king asked the mowers to whom the field on which they were at work belonged.

"It is the property of the marquis of Carabas," they all cried with one voice, for the threat from Puss had frightened them.

"You have inherited a fine estate," the king remarked to Carabas.

"As you see for yourself, Sire," replied the marquis; "this is a meadow which never fails to yield an abundant crop each year."

Still travelling ahead, the cat came upon some harvesters.

"Listen, my good fellows," said he; "if you do not declare that every one of these fields belongs to the marquis of Carabas, you will all be chopped up into little bits like mincemeat."

The king came by a moment later, and wished to know who was the owner of the fields in sight.

"It is the marquis of Carabas," cried the harvesters.

At this the king was more pleased than ever with the marquis.

Preceding the coach on its journey, the cat made the same threat to all whom he met, and the king grew astonished at the great wealth of the marquis of Carabas.

Finally Master Puss reached a splendid castle, which belonged to an ogre. He was the richest ogre that had ever been known, for all the lands through which the king had passed were part of the castle domain.

The cat had taken care to find out who this ogre was, and what powers he possessed. He now asked for an interview, declaring that he was unwilling to pass so close to the castle without having the honour of paying his respects to the owner.

The ogre received him as civilly as an ogre can, and

bade him sit down.

"I have been told," said Puss, "that you have the power to change yourself into any kind of animal – for example, that you can transform yourself into a lion or an elephant."

"That is perfectly true," said the ogre, curtly; "and just to prove it you shall see me turn into a lion."

Puss was so frightened on seeing a lion before him that he sprang on to the roof – not without difficulty and danger, for his boots were not meant for walking on tiles.

Perceiving presently that the ogre had abandoned his transformation, Puss descended, and owned to having been thoroughly frightened.

"I have also been told," he added, "but I can scarcely believe it, that you have the further power to take the shape of the smallest animals – for example, that you can change yourself into a rat or a mouse. I confess that to me it seems quite impossible."

"Impossible?" cried the ogre; "you shall see!" And in the same moment he changed himself into a mouse, which began to run about the floor. No sooner did Puss see it than he pounced on it and ate it.

Presently the king came along, and noticing the ogre's beautiful mansion desired to visit it. The cat heard the rumble of the coach as it crossed the castle drawbridge, and running out to the courtyard cried to the king:

"Welcome, your Majesty, to the castle of the marquis of Carabas!"

"What's that?" cried the king. "Is this castle also yours, marquis? Nothing could be finer than this court-yard and the buildings which I see all about. With your permission we will go inside and look round."

The marquis gave his hand to the young princess, and followed the king as he led the way up the staircase. Entering a great hall they found there a magnificent collation. This had been prepared by the ogre for some friends who were to pay him a visit that very day. The latter had not dared to enter when they learned that the king was there.

The king was now quite as charmed with the excellent qualities of the marquis of Carabas as his daughter. The latter was completely captivated by him. Noting the great wealth of which the marquis was evidently possessed, and having quaffed several cups of wine, he turned to his host, saying:

"It rests with you, marquis, whether you will be my son-in-law."

The marquis, bowing very low, accepted the honour which the king bestowed upon him. The very same day he married the princess.

Puss became a personage of great importance, and gave up hunting mice, except for amusement.

MORAL

*No matter how great may be the advantages
Of enjoying a rich inheritance,*

Coming down from father to son,
Most young people will do well to remember
That industry, knowledge and a clever mind
Are worth more than mere gifts from others.

ANOTHER MORAL

If a miller's son, in so short a time,
Can win the heart of a Princess,
So that she gazes at him with lovelorn eyes,
Perhaps it is the clothes, the appearance,
and youthfulness
That are seldom the indifferent means
Of inspiring love!

Little Tom Thumb

ONCE UPON A TIME there lived a wood-cutter and his wife, who had seven children, all boys. The eldest was only ten years old, and the youngest was seven. People were astonished that the wood-cutter had so many children in so short a time, but the reason was that his wife delighted in children, and never had less than two at a time.

They were very poor, and their seven children were a great tax on them, for none of them was yet able to earn his own living. And they were troubled also because the youngest was very delicate and could not speak a word. They mistook for stupidity what was in reality a mark of good sense.

The youngest boy was very little. At his birth he was scarcely bigger than a man's thumb, and he was called in consequence "Little Tom Thumb." The poor child was the scapegoat of the family, and got the blame for everything. All the same, he was the sharpest and shrewdest of the brothers, and if he spoke but little he listened much.

There came a very bad year, when the famine was so great that these poor people resolved to get rid of their family. One evening, after the children had gone to bed, the wood-cutter was sitting in the chimney-corner with his wife. His heart was heavy with sorrow as he said to her:

"It must be plain enough to you that we can no longer feed our children. I cannot see them die of hunger before my eyes, and I have made up my mind to take them tomorrow to the forest and lose them there. It will be easy enough to manage, for while they are amusing themselves by collecting faggots we have only to disappear without their seeing us."

"Ah!" cried the wood-cutter's wife, "do you mean to say you are capable of letting your own children be lost?"

In vain did her husband remind her of their terrible poverty; she could not agree. She was poor, but she was their mother. In the end, however, reflecting what a grief it would be to see them die of hunger, she consented to the plan, and went weeping to bed.

Little Tom Thumb had heard all that was said. Having discovered, when in bed, that serious talk was going on, he had got up softly, and had slipped under his father's stool in order to listen without being seen. He went back to bed, but did not sleep a wink for the rest of the night, thinking over what he had better do. In the morning he rose very early and went to the edge of a brook. There he filled his pockets with little white pebbles and came quickly home again.

They all set out, and little Tom Thumb said not a word to his brothers of what he knew.

They went into a forest which was so dense that when only ten paces apart they could not see each other. The wood-cutter set about his work, and the children began to collect twigs to make faggots. Presently the father and mother, seeing them busy at their task, edged gradually away, and then hurried off in haste along a little narrow footpath.

When the children found they were alone they began to cry and call out with all their might. Little Tom Thumb let them cry, being confident that they would get back home again. For on the way he had dropped the little white stones which he carried in his pocket all along the path.

"Don't be afraid, brothers," he said presently; "our parents have left us here, but I will take you home again. Just follow me."

They fell in behind him, and he led them straight to their house by the same path which they had taken to the forest. At first they dared not go in, but placed themselves against the door, where they could hear everything their father and mother were saying.

Now the wood-cutter and his wife had no sooner reached home than the lord of the manor sent them a sum of ten crowns which had been owing from him for a long time, and of which they had given up hope. This put new life into them, for the poor creatures were dying of hunger.

The wood-cutter sent his wife off to the butcher at once, and as it was such a long time since they had had anything to eat, she bought three times as much meat as a supper for two required.

When they found themselves once more at table, the wood-cutter's wife began to lament.

"Alas! where are our poor children now?" she said; "they could make a good meal off what we have over. Mind you, William, it was you who wished to lose them: I declared over and over again that we should repent it. What are they doing now in that forest? Merciful heavens, perhaps the wolves have already eaten them! A monster you must be to lose your children in this way!"

At last the wood-cutter lost patience, for she repeated more than twenty times that he would repent it, and that she had told him so. He threatened to beat her if she did not hold her tongue.

It was not that the wood-cutter was less grieved than his wife, but she browbeat him, and he was of the same opinion as many other people, who like a woman to have the knack of saying the right thing, but not the trick of being always in the right.

"Alas!" cried the wood-cutter's wife, bursting into tears, "where are now my children, my poor children?"

She said it once so loud that the children at the door heard it plainly. Together they all called out:

"Here we are! Here we are!"

She rushed to open the door for them, and exclaimed, as she embraced them:

"How glad I am to see you again, dear children! You must be very tired and very hungry. And you, Peterkin, how muddy you are – come and let me wash you!"

This Peterkin was her eldest son. She loved him more than all the others because he was inclined to be red-headed, and she herself was rather red.

They sat down at the table and ate with an appetite which it did their parents good to see. They all talked at once, as they recounted the fears they had felt in the forest.

The good souls were delighted to have their children with them again, and the pleasure continued as long as the ten crowns lasted. But when the money was all spent they relapsed into their former sadness. They again resolved to lose the children, and to lead them much further away than they had done the first time, so as to do the job thoroughly. But though they were careful not to speak openly about it, their conversation did not escape little Tom Thumb, who made up his mind to get out of the situation as he had done on the former occasion.

But though he got up early to go and collect his little stones, he found the door of the house doubly locked, and he could not carry out his plan.

He could not think what to do until the wood-cutter's wife gave them each a piece of bread for breakfast. Then it occurred to him to use the bread in place of the stones, by throwing crumbs along the path which they took, and he tucked it tight in his pocket.

Their parents led them into the thickest and darkest part of the forest, and as soon as they were there slipped away by a side-path and left them. This did not much trouble little Tom Thumb, for he believed he could easily find the way back by means of the bread which he had scattered wherever he walked. But to his dismay he could not discover a single crumb. The birds had come along and eaten it all.

They were in sore trouble now, for with every step they strayed further, and became more and more entangled in the forest. Night came on and a terrific wind arose, which filled them with dreadful alarm. On every side they seemed to hear nothing but the howling of wolves which were coming to eat them up. They dared not speak or move.

In addition it began to rain so heavily that they were soaked to the skin. At every step they tripped and fell on the wet ground, getting up again covered with mud, not knowing what to do with their hands.

Little Tom Thumb climbed to the top of a tree, in an endeavour to see something. Looking all about him he espied, far away on the other side of the forest, a little light like that of a candle. He got down from the tree, and was terribly disappointed to find that when he was on the ground he could see nothing at all.

After they had walked some distance in the direction of the light, however, he caught a glimpse of it again as they were nearing the edge of the forest. At last they reached the house where the light was burning, but not without much anxiety, for every time they had to go down into a hollow they lost sight of it.

They knocked at the door, and a good dame opened to them. She asked them what they wanted.

Little Tom Thumb explained that they were poor children who had lost their way in the forest, and begged her, for pity's sake, to give them a night's lodging.

Noticing what bonny children they all were, the woman began to cry.

"Alas, my poor little dears!" she said; "you do not know the place you have come to! Have you not heard that this is the house of an ogre who eats little children?"

"Alas, madam!" answered little Tom Thumb, trembling like all the rest of his brothers, "what shall we do? One thing is very certain: if you do not take us in, the wolves of the forest will devour us this very night, and that being so we should prefer to be eaten by your husband. Perhaps he may take pity on us, if you will plead for us."

The ogre's wife, thinking she might be able to hide them from her husband till the next morning, allowed them to come in, and put them to warm near a huge fire, where a whole sheep was cooking on the spit for the ogre's supper.

Just as they were beginning to get warm they heard two or three great bangs at the door. The ogre had returned. His wife hid them quickly under the bed and ran to open the door.

The first thing the ogre did was to ask whether supper

was ready and the wine opened. Then without ado he sat down to table. Blood was still dripping from the sheep, but it seemed all the better to him for that. He sniffed to right and left, declaring that he could smell fresh flesh.

"Indeed!" said his wife. "It must be the calf which I have just dressed that you smell."

"I smell fresh flesh, I tell you," shouted the ogre, eyeing his wife askance; "and there is something going on here which I do not understand."

With these words he got up from the table and went straight to the bed.

"Aha!" said he; "so this is the way you deceive me, wicked woman that you are! I have a great mind to eat you too! It's lucky for you that you are old and tough! I am expecting three ogre friends of mine to pay me a visit in the next few days, and here is a tasty dish which will just come in nicely for them!"

One after another he dragged the children out from under the bed.

The poor things threw themselves on their knees, imploring mercy; but they had to deal with the most cruel of all ogres. Far from pitying them, he was already devouring them with his eyes, and repeating to his wife that when cooked with a good sauce they would make most dainty morsels.

Off he went to get a large knife, which he sharpened, as he drew near the poor children, on a long stone in his left hand.

He had already seized one of them when his wife called out to him. "What do you want to do it now for?" she said; "will it not be time enough to-morrow?"

"Hold your tongue," replied the ogre; "they will be all the more tender."

"But you have such a lot of meat," rejoined his wife; "look, there are a calf, two sheep, and half a pig."

"You are right," said the ogre; "give them a good supper to fatten them up, and take them to bed."

The good woman was overjoyed and brought them a splendid supper; but the poor little wretches were so cowed with fright they could not eat.

As for the ogre, he went back to his drinking, very pleased to have such good entertainment for his friends. He drank a dozen cups more than usual, and was obliged to go off to bed early, for the wine had gone somewhat to his head.

Now the ogre had seven daughters who as yet were only children. These little ogresses all had the most lovely complexions, for, like their father, they ate fresh meat. But they had little round grey eyes, crooked noses, and very large mouths, with long and exceedingly sharp teeth, set far apart. They were not so very wicked at present, but they showed great promise, for already they were in the habit of killing little children to suck their blood.

They had gone to bed early, and were all seven in a great bed, each with a crown of gold upon her head.

In the same room there was another bed, equally

large. Into this the ogre's wife put the seven little boys, and then went to sleep herself beside her husband.

Little Tom Thumb was fearful lest the ogre should suddenly regret that he had not cut the throats of himself and his brothers the evening before. Having noticed that the ogre's daughters all had golden crowns upon their heads, he got up in the middle of the night and softly placed his own cap and those of his brothers on their heads. Before doing so, he carefully removed the crowns of gold, putting them on his own and his brothers' heads. In this way, if the ogre were to feel like slaughtering them that night he would mistake the girls for the boys, and vice versa.

Things fell out just as he had anticipated. The ogre, waking up at midnight, regretted that he had postponed till the morrow what he could have done overnight. Jumping briskly out of bed, he seized his knife, crying: "Now then, let's see how the little rascals are; we won't make the same mistake twice!"

He groped his way up to his daughters' room, and approached the bed in which were the seven little boys. All were sleeping, with the exception of little Tom Thumb, who was numb with fear when he felt the ogre's hand, as it touched the head of each brother in turn, reach his own.

"Upon my word," said the ogre, as he felt the golden crowns; "a nice job I was going to make of it! It is very evident that I drank a little too much last night!"

Forthwith he went to the bed where his daughters

were, and here he felt the little boys' caps.

"Aha, here are the little scamps!" he cried; "now for a smart bit of work!"

With these words, and without a moment's hesitation, he cut the throats of his seven daughters, and well satisfied with his work went back to bed beside his wife.

No sooner did little Tom Thumb hear him snoring than he woke up his brothers, bidding them dress quickly and follow him. They crept quietly down to the garden, and jumped from the wall. All through the night they ran in haste and terror, without the least idea of where they were going.

When the ogre woke up he said to his wife:

"Go upstairs and dress those little rascals who were here last night."

The ogre's wife was astonished at her husband's kindness, never doubting that he meant her to go and put on their clothes. She went upstairs, and was horrified to discover her seven daughters bathed in blood, with their throats cut.

She fell at once into a swoon, which is the way of most women in similar circumstances.

The ogre, thinking his wife was very long in carrying out his orders, went up to help her and was no less astounded than his wife at the terrible spectacle which confronted him.

"What's this I have done?" he exclaimed. "I will be revenged on the wretches, and quickly, too!"

He threw a jugful of water over his wife's face, and

having brought her round ordered her to fetch his seven-league boots, so that he might overtake the children.

He set off over the countryside, and strode far and wide until he came to the road along which the poor children were travelling. They were not more than a few yards from their home when they saw the ogre striding from hill-top to hill-top, and stepping over rivers as though they were merely tiny streams.

Little Tom Thumb espied near at hand a cave in some rocks. In this he hid his brothers, and himself followed them in, while continuing to keep a watchful eye upon the movements of the ogre.

Now the ogre was feeling very tired after so much fruitless marching (for seven-league boots are very fatiguing to their wearer), and felt like taking a little rest. As it happened, he went and sat down on the very rock beneath which the little boys were hiding. Overcome with weariness, he had not sat there long before he fell asleep and began to snore so terribly that the poor children were as frightened as when he had held his great knife to their throats.

Little Tom Thumb was not so alarmed. He told his brothers to flee at once to their home while the ogre was still sleeping soundly, and not to worry about him. They took his advice and ran quickly home.

Little Tom Thumb now approached the ogre and gently pulled off his boots, which he at once donned himself. The boots were very heavy and very large, but being enchanted boots they had the faculty of growing larger or smaller according to the leg they had to suit. Consequently they always fitted as though they had been made for the wearer.

He went straight to the ogre's house, where he found the ogre's wife weeping over her murdered daughters.

"Your husband," said little Tom Thumb, "is in great danger, for he has been captured by a gang of thieves, and the latter have sworn to kill him if he does not hand over all his gold and silver. Just as they had the dagger at his throat, he caught sight of me and begged me to come to you and thus rescue him from his terrible plight. You are to give me everything of value which he possesses, without keeping back a thing, otherwise he will be slain without mercy. As the matter is urgent he wished me to wear his seven-league boots, to save time, and also to prove to you that I am no imposter."

The ogre's wife, in great alarm, gave him immediately all that she had, for although this was an ogre who devoured little children, he was by no means a bad husband.

Little Tom Thumb, laden with all the ogre's wealth, forthwith repaired to his father's house, where he was received with great joy.

* * * *

Many people do not agree about this last adventure, and pretend that little Tom Thumb never committed this theft from the ogre, and only took the seven-league boots, about which he had no compunction, since they were only used by the ogre for catching little children. These folks assert that they are in a position to know, having been guests at the wood-cutter's cottage. They further say that when little Tom Thumb had put on the ogre's boots, he went off to the Court, where he knew there was great anxiety concerning the result of a battle which was being fought by an army two hundred leagues away.

They say that he went to the king and undertook, if desired, to bring news of the army before the day was out; and that the king promised him a large sum of money if he could carry out his project.

Little Tom Thumb brought news that very night, and this first errand having brought him into notice, he made as much money as he wished. For not only did the king pay him handsomely to carry orders to the army, but many ladies at the court gave him anything he asked to get them news of their lovers, and this was his greatest source of income. He was occasionally entrusted by wives with letters to their husbands, but they paid him so badly, and this branch of the business brought him in so little, that he did not even bother to reckon what he made from it.

After acting as courier for some time, and amassing great wealth thereby, little Tom Thumb returned to his father's house, and was there greeted with the greatest joy imaginable. He made all his family comfortable, buying newly-created positions for his father and brothers. In this way he set them all up, not forgetting at the same time to look well after himself.

MORAL

Having many children seldom brings unhappiness,
Especially if they are attractive, well-bred and strong;
But if one is sickly or is slow of wit,
How often is he despised, jeered at and scorned!
Although sometimes it is this oddest one
Who brings good fortune to all the family!

The Fairies

ONCE UPON A TIME there lived a widow with two daughters. The elder was often mistaken for her mother, so like her was she both in nature and in looks; parent and child being so disagreeable and arrogant that no one could live with them.

The younger girl, who took after her father in the gentleness and sweetness of her disposition, was also one of the prettiest girls imaginable. The mother doted on the elder daughter – naturally enough, since she resembled her so closely – and disliked the younger one as intensely. She made the latter live in the kitchen and work hard from morning till night.

One of the poor child's many duties was to go twice a day and draw water from a spring a good half-mile away, bringing it back in a large pitcher. One day when she was at the spring an old woman came up and begged for a drink.

"Why, certainly, good mother," the pretty lass replied. Rinsing her pitcher, she drew some water from the cleanest part of the spring and handed it to the dame, lifting up the jug so that she might drink the more easily.

Now this old woman was a fairy, who had taken the form of a poor village dame to see just how far the girl's good nature would go. "You are so pretty," she said, when she had finished drinking, "and so polite, that I am determined to bestow a gift upon you. This is the boon I grant you: with every word that you utter there shall fall from your mouth either a flower or a precious stone."

When the girl reached home she was scolded by her mother for being so long in coming back from the spring.

"I am sorry to have been so long, mother," said the poor child.

As she spoke these words there fell from her mouth three roses, three pearls, and three diamonds.

"What's this?" cried her mother; "did I see pearls and diamonds dropping out of your mouth? What does this mean, dear daughter?" (This was the first time she had ever addressed her daughter affectionately.)

The poor child told a simple tale of what had happened, and in speaking scattered diamonds right and left.

"Really," said her mother, "I must send my own child there. Come here, Fanchon; look what comes out of your sister's mouth whenever she speaks! Wouldn't you like to be able to do the same? All you have to do is to go and draw some water at the spring, and when a poor woman asks you for a drink, give it her very nicely."

"Oh, indeed!" replied the ill-mannered girl; "don't you wish you may see me going there!"

"I tell you that you are to go," said her mother, "and

to go this instant."

Very sulkily the girl went off, taking with her the best silver flagon in the house. No sooner had she reached the spring than she saw a lady, magnificently attired, who came towards her from the forest, and asked for a drink. This was the same fairy who had appeared to her sister, masquerading now as a princess in order to see how far this girl's ill-nature would carry her.

"Do you think I have come here just to get you a drink?" said the loutish damsel, arrogantly. "I suppose you think I brought a silver flagon here specially for that purpose – it's so likely, isn't it? Drink from the spring, if you want to!"

"You are not very polite," said the fairy, displaying no sign of anger. "Well, in return for your lack of courtesy I decree that for every word you utter a snake or a toad shall drop out of your mouth."

The moment her mother caught sight of her coming back she cried out, "Well, daughter?"

"Well, mother?" replied the rude girl. As she spoke a viper and a toad were spat out of her mouth.

"Gracious heavens!" cried her mother; "what do I see? Her sister is the cause of this, and I will make her pay for it!"

Off she ran to thrash the poor child, but the latter fled away and hid in the forest near by. The king's son met her on his way home from hunting and, noticing how pretty she was, inquired what she was doing all alone, and what she was weeping about.

"Alas, sir," she cried; "my mother has driven me from home!"

As she spoke the prince saw four or five pearls and as many diamonds fall from her mouth. He begged her to tell him how this came about, and she told him the whole story.

The king's son fell in love with her, and reflecting that such a gift as had been bestowed upon her was worth more than any dowry which another maiden might bring him, he took her to the palace of his royal father, and there married her.

As for the sister, she made herself so hateful that even her mother drove her out of the house. Nowhere could the wretched girl find any one who would take her in, and at last she lay down in the forest and died.

MORAL

Diamonds and golden coins
Can do great things for our spirits.
Kind words, nevertheless, Have still greater influence
And are in themselves a richer treasure.

ANOTHER MORAL

Kindness sometimes involves a little trouble
And taking pains to be considerate,
But sooner or later it has its reward
And often at a moment when it's least expected.

Ricky of the Tuft

ONCE UPON A TIME there was a queen who bore a son so ugly and misshapen that for some time it was doubtful if he would have human form at all. But a fairy who was present at his birth promised that he should have plenty of brains, and added that by virtue of the gift which she had just bestowed upon him he would be able to impart to the person whom he should love best the same degree of intelligence which he possessed himself.

This somewhat consoled the poor queen, who was greatly disappointed at having brought into the world such a hideous brat. And indeed, no sooner did the child begin to speak than his sayings proved to be full of shrewdness, while all that he did was somehow so clever that he charmed every one.

I forgot to mention that when he was born he had a little tuft of hair upon his head. For this reason he was called Ricky of the Tuft, Ricky being his family name.

Some seven or eight years later the queen of a neighbouring kingdom gave birth to twin daughters.

The first one to come into the world was more beautiful than the dawn, and the queen was so overjoyed that it was feared her great excitement might do her some harm. The same fairy who had assisted at the birth of Ricky of the Tuft was present, and, in order to moderate the transports of the queen she declared that this little princess would have no sense at all, and would be as stupid as she was beautiful.

The queen was deeply mortified, and a moment or two later her chagrin became greater still, for the second daughter proved to be extremely ugly.

"Do not be distressed, Madam," said the fairy; "your daughter shall be recompensed in another way. She shall have so much good sense that her lack of beauty will scarcely be noticed."

"May Heaven grant it!" said the queen; "but is there no means by which the elder, who is so beautiful, can be endowed with some intelligence?"

"In the matter of brains I can do nothing for her, Madam," said the fairy, "but as regards beauty I can do a great deal. As there is nothing I would not do to please you, I will bestow upon her the power of making beautiful any person who shall greatly please her."

As the two princesses grew up their perfections increased, and everywhere the beauty of the elder and the wit of the younger were the subject of common talk.

It is equally true that their defects also increased as they became older. The younger grew uglier every minute, and the elder daily became more stupid.

Either she answered nothing at all when spoken to, or replied with some idiotic remark. At the same time she was so awkward that she could not set four china vases on the mantelpiece without breaking one of them, nor drink a glass of water without spilling half of it over her clothes.

Now although the elder girl possessed the great advantage which beauty always confers upon youth, she was nevertheless outshone in almost all company by her younger sister. At first every one gathered round the beauty to see and admire her, but very soon they were all attracted by the graceful and easy conversation of the clever one. In a very short time the elder girl would be left entirely alone, while everybody clustered round her sister.

The elder princess was not so stupid that she was not aware of this, and she would willingly have surrendered all her beauty for half her sister's cleverness. Sometimes she was ready to die of grief, for the queen, though a sensible woman, could not refrain from occasionally reproaching her with her stupidity.

The princess had retired one day to a wood to bemoan her misfortune, when she saw approaching her an ugly little man, of very disagreeable appearance, but clad in magnificent attire.

This was the young prince, Ricky of the Tuft. He had fallen in love with her portrait, which was everywhere to be seen, and had left his father's kingdom in order to have the pleasure of seeing and talking to her.

Delighted to meet her thus alone, he approached with every mark of respect and politeness. But while he paid her the usual compliments he noticed that she was plunged in melancholy.

"I cannot understand, madam," he said, "how any one with your beauty can be so sad as you appear. I can boast of having seen many fair ladies, and I declare that none of them could compare in beauty with you."

"It is very kind of you to say so, sir," answered the princess; and stopped there, at a loss what to say further.

"Beauty," said Ricky, "is of such great advantage that everything else can be disregarded; and I do not see that the possessor of it can have anything much to grieve about."

To this the princess replied:

"I would rather be as plain as you are and have some sense, than be as beautiful as I am and at the same time stupid."

"Nothing more clearly displays good sense, madam, than a belief that one is not possessed of it. It follows, therefore, that the more one has, the more one fears it to be wanting."

"I am not sure about that," said the princess; "but I know only too well that I am very stupid, and this is the reason of the misery which is nearly killing me."

"If that is all that troubles you, madam, I can easily put an end to your suffering."

"How will you manage that?" said the princess.

"I am able, madam," said Ricky of the Tuft, "to

bestow as much good sense as it is possible to possess on the person whom I love the most. You are that person, and it therefore rests with you to decide whether you will acquire so much intelligence. The only condition is that you shall consent to marry me."

The princess was dumbfounded, and remained silent.

"I can see," pursued Ricky, "that this suggestion perplexes you, and I am not surprised. But I will give you a whole year to make up your mind to it."

The princess had so little sense, and at the same time desired it so ardently, that she persuaded herself the end of this year would never come. So she accepted the offer which had been made to her. No sooner had she given her word to Ricky that she would marry him within one year from that very day, than she felt a complete change come over her. She found herself able to say all that she wished with the greatest ease, and to say it in an elegant, finished, and natural manner. She at once engaged Ricky in a brilliant and lengthy conversation, holding her own so well that Ricky feared he had given her a larger share of sense than he had retained for himself.

On her return to the palace amazement reigned throughout the Court at such a sudden and extraordinary change. Whereas formerly they had been accustomed to hear her give vent to silly, pert remarks, they now heard her express herself sensibly and very wittily.

The entire Court was overjoyed. The only person not too pleased was the younger sister, for now that she had no longer the advantage over the elder in wit, she seemed nothing but a little fright in comparison.

The king himself often took her advice, and several times held his councils in her apartment.

The news of this change spread abroad, and the princes of the neighbouring kingdoms made many attempts to captivate her. Almost all asked her in marriage. But she found none with enough sense, and so she listened to all without promising herself to any.

At last came one who was so powerful, so rich, so witty, and so handsome, that she could not help being somewhat attracted by him. Her father noticed this, and told her she could make her own choice of a husband: she had only to declare herself.

Now the more sense one has, the more difficult it is to make up one's mind in an affair of this kind. After thanking her father, therefore, she asked for a little time to think it over.

In order to ponder quietly what she had better do she went to walk in a wood – the very one, as it happened, where she encountered Ricky of the Tuft.

While she walked, deep in thought, she heard beneath her feet a thudding sound, as though many people were running busily to and fro. Listening more attentively she heard voices. "Bring me that boiler," said one; then another – "Put some wood on that fire!"

At that moment the ground opened, and she saw below what appeared to be a large kitchen full of cooks and scullions, and all the train of attendants which the preparation of a great banquet involves. A gang of some twenty or thirty spit-turners emerged and took up their positions round a very long table in a path in the wood. They all wore their cook's caps on one side, and with their basting implements in their hands they kept time together as they worked, to the lilt of a melodious song.

The princess was astonished by this spectacle, and asked for whom their work was being done.

"For Prince Ricky of the Tuft, madam," said the fore-man of the gang; "his wedding is to-morrow."

At this the princess was more surprised than ever. In a flash she remembered that it was a year to the very day since she had promised to marry Prince Ricky of the Tuft, and was taken aback by the recollection. The reason she had forgotten was that when she made the promise she was still without sense, and with the acquisition of that intelligence which the prince had bestowed upon her, all memory of her former stupidities had been blotted out.

She had not gone another thirty paces when Ricky of the Tuft appeared before her, gallant and resplendent, like a prince upon his wedding day.

"As you see, madam," he said, "I keep my word to the minute. I do not doubt that you have come to keep yours, and by giving me your hand to make me the happiest of men."

"I will be frank with you," replied the princess. "I have not yet made up my mind on the point, and I am afraid I shall never be able to take the decision you desire."

"You astonish me, madam," said Ricky of the Tuft.

"I can believe it," said the princess, "and undoubtedly, if I had to deal with a clown, or a man who lacked good sense, I should feel myself very awkwardly situated. 'A princess must keep her word,' he would say, 'and you must marry me because you promised to!' But I am speaking to a man of the world, of the greatest good sense, and I am sure that he will listen to reason. As you are aware, I could not make up my mind to marry you even when I was entirely without sense; how can you expect that to-day, possessing the intelligence you bestowed on me, which makes me still more difficult to please than formerly, I should take a decision which I could not take then? If you wished so much to marry me, you were very wrong to relieve me of my stupidity, and to let me see more clearly than I did."

"If a man who lacked good sense," replied Ricky of the Tuft, "would be justified, as you have just said, in reproaching you for breaking your word, why do you expect, madam, that I should act differently where the happiness of my whole life is at stake? Is it reasonable that people who have sense should be treated worse than those who have none? Would you maintain that for a moment – you, who so markedly have sense, and desired so ardently to have it? But, pardon me, let us get to the facts. With the exception of my ugliness, is there anything about me which displeases you? Are you dissatisfied with my breeding, my brains, my disposition, or my manners?"

"In no way," replied the princess; "I like exceedingly

all that you have displayed of the qualities you mention."

"In that case," said Ricky of the Tuft, "happiness will be mine, for it lies in your power to make me the most attractive of men."

"How can that be done?" asked the princess.

"It will happen of itself," replied Ricky of the Tuft, "if you love me well enough to wish that it be so. To remove your doubts, madam, let me tell you that the same fairy who on the day of my birth bestowed upon me the power of endowing with intelligence the woman of my choice, gave to you also the power of endowing with beauty the man whom you should love, and on whom you should wish to confer this favour."

"If that is so," said the princess, "I wish with all my heart that you may become the handsomest and most attractive prince in the world, and I give you without reserve the boon which it is mine to bestow."

No sooner had the princess uttered these words than Ricky of the Tuft appeared before her eyes as the handsomest, most graceful and attractive man that she had ever set eyes on.

Some people assert that this was not the work of fairy enchantment, but that love alone brought about the transformation. They say that the princess, as she mused upon her lover's constancy, upon his good sense, and his many admirable qualities of heart and head, grew blind to the deformity of his body and the ugliness of his face; that his hump back seemed no more than was natural in a man who could make the courtliest of bows, and that the dreadful limp which had formerly distressed her now betokened nothing more than a certain diffidence and charming deference of manner. They say further that she found his eyes shone all the brighter for their squint, and that this defect in them was to her but a sign of passionate love; while his great red nose she found nought but martial and heroic.

However that may be, the princess promised to marry him on the spot, provided only that he could obtain the consent of her royal father.

The king knew Ricky of the Tuft to be a prince both wise and witty, and on learning of his daughter's regard for him, he accepted him with pleasure as a son-in-law.

The wedding took place upon the morrow, just as Ricky of the Tuft had foreseen, and in accordance with the arrangements he had long ago planned and brought about.

MORAL

That which you see written here
Is less a story than the truth itself.
Everything is beautiful in the one we love
And all that we love has beauty.

ANOTHER MORAL

In one whom Nature has blessed with beautiful disposition,
And whose living portrait has that which Art can never match;
All these gifts have less effect in touching a heart than a single
Invisible charm which love alone knows how to discover.

Cinderella

O NCE UPON A TIME there was a worthy man who married for his second wife the haughtiest, proudest woman that had ever been seen. She had two daughters, who possessed their mother's temper and resembled her in everything. Her husband, on the other hand, had a young daughter, who was of an exceptionally sweet and gentle nature. She got this from her mother, who had been the nicest person in the world.

The wedding was no sooner over than the stepmother began to display her bad temper. She could not endure the excellent qualities of this young girl, for they made her own daughters appear more hateful than ever. She thrust upon her all the meanest tasks about the house. It was she who had to clean the plates and the stairs, and sweep out the rooms of the mistress of the house and her daughters. She slept on a wretched mattress in a garret at the top of the house, while the sisters had rooms with parquet flooring, and beds of the most fashionable style, with mirrors in which they could see themselves from top to toe.

The poor girl endured everything patiently, not daring to complain to her father. The latter would have scolded her, because he was entirely ruled by his wife. When she had finished her work she used to sit amongst the cinders in the corner of the chimney, and it was from this habit that she came to be commonly known as Cinder-clod. The younger of the two sisters, who was not quite so spiteful as the elder, called her Cinderella. But her wretched clothes did not prevent Cinderella from being a hundred times more beautiful than her sisters, for all their resplendent garments.

It happened that the king's son gave a ball, and he invited all persons of high degree. The two young ladies were invited amongst others, for they cut a considerable figure in the country. Not a little pleased were they, and the question of what clothes and what mode of dressing the hair would become them best took up all their time. And all this meant fresh trouble for Cinderella, for it was she who went over her sisters' linen and ironed their ruffles. They could talk of nothing else but the fashions in clothes.

"For my part," said the elder, "I shall wear my dress of red velvet, with the Honiton lace."

"I have only my everyday petticoat," said the younger, "but to make up for it I shall wear my cloak with the golden flowers and my necklace of diamonds, which are not so bad."

They sent for a good hairdresser to arrange their double-frilled caps, and bought patches at the best shop.

They summoned Cinderella and asked her advice, for she had good taste. Cinderella gave them the best possible suggestions, and even offered to dress their hair, to which they gladly agreed.

While she was thus occupied they said:

"Cinderella, would you not like to go to the ball?"

"Ah, but you fine young ladies are laughing at me. It would be no place for me."

"That is very true, people would laugh to see a cinder-clod in the ballroom."

Any one else but Cinderella would have done their hair amiss, but she was good-natured, and she finished them off to perfection. They were so excited in their glee that for nearly two days they ate nothing. They broke more than a dozen laces through drawing their stays tight in order to make their waists more slender, and they were perpetually in front of a mirror.

At last the happy day arrived. Away they went, Cinderella watching them as long as she could keep them in sight. When she could no longer see them she began to cry. Her godmother found her in tears, and asked what was troubling her.

"I should like – I should like – "

She was crying so bitterly that she could not finish the sentence.

Said her godmother, who was a fairy:

"You would like to go to the ball, would you not?"

"Ah, yes," said Cinderella, sighing.

"Well, well," said her godmother, "promise to be a

good girl and I will arrange for you to go."

She took Cinderella into her room and said:

"Go into the garden and bring me a pumpkin."

Cinderella went at once and gathered the finest that she could find. This she brought to her godmother, wondering how a pumpkin could help in taking her to the ball.

Her godmother scooped it out, and when only the rind was left, struck it with her wand. Instantly the pumpkin was changed into a beautiful coach, gilded all over.

Then she went and looked in the mouse-trap, where she found six mice all alive. She told Cinderella to lift the door of the mouse-trap a little, and as each mouse came out she gave it a tap with her wand, whereupon it was transformed into a fine horse. So that here was a fine team of six dappled mouse-grey horses.

But she was puzzled to know how to provide a coachman.

"I will go and see," said Cinderella, "if there is not rat in the rat-trap. We could make a coachman of him."

"Quite right," said her godmother, "go and see."

Cinderella brought in the rat-trap, which contained three big rats. The fairy chose one specially on account of his elegant whiskers.

As soon as she had touched him he turned into a fat coachman with the finest moustachios that ever were seen.

"Now go into the garden and bring me the six lizards which you will find behind the water-butt."

No sooner had they been brought than the

godmother turned them into six lackeys, who at once climbed up behind the coach in their braided liveries, and hung on there as if they had never done anything else all their lives.

Then said the fairy godmother:

"Well, there you have the means of going to the ball. Are you satisfied?"

"Oh, yes, but am I to go like this in my ugly clothes?"

Her godmother merely touched her with her wand, and on the instant her clothes were changed into garments of gold and silver cloth, bedecked with jewels. After that her godmother gave her a pair of glass slippers, the prettiest in the world.

Thus altered, she entered the coach. Her godmother bade her not to stay beyond midnight whatever happened, warning her that if she remained at the ball a moment longer, her coach would again become a pumpkin, her horses mice, and her lackeys lizards, while her old clothes would reappear upon her once more.

She promised her godmother that she would not fail to leave the ball before midnight, and away she went, beside herself with delight.

The king's son, when he was told of the arrival of a great princess whom nobody knew, went forth to receive her. He handed her down from the coach, and led her into the hall where the company was assembled. At once there fell a great silence. The dancers stopped, the violins played no more, so rapt was the attention which everybody bestowed upon the superb beauty of the unknown guest. Everywhere could be heard in confused whispers:

"Oh, how beautiful she is!"

The king, old man as he was, could not take his eyes off her, and whispered to the queen that it was many a long day since he had seen any one so beautiful and charming.

All the ladies were eager to scrutinise her clothes and the dressing of her hair, being determined to copy them on the morrow, provided they could find materials so fine, and tailors so clever.

The king's son placed her in the seat of honour, and at once begged the privilege of being her partner in a dance. Such was the grace with which she danced that the admiration of all was increased.

A magnificent supper was served, but the young prince could eat nothing, so taken up was he with watching her. She went and sat beside her sisters, and bestowed numberless attentions upon them. She made them share with her the oranges and lemons which the king had given her – greatly to their astonishment, for they did not recognise her.

While they were talking, Cinderella heard the clock strike a quarter to twelve. She at once made a profound curtsey to the company, and departed as quickly as she could.

As soon as she was home again she sought out her godmother, and having thanked her, declared that she wished to go upon the morrow once more to the ball, because the king's son had invited her.

While she was busy telling her godmother all that had happened at the ball, her two sisters knocked at the door. Cinderella let them in.

"What a long time you have been in coming!" she declared, rubbing her eyes and stretching herself as if she had only just awakened. In real truth she had not for a moment wished to sleep since they had left.

"If you had been at the ball," said one of the sisters, "you would not be feeling weary. There came a most beautiful princess, the most beautiful that has ever been seen, and she bestowed numberless attentions upon us, and gave us her oranges and lemons."

Cinderella was overjoyed. She asked them the name of the princess, but they replied that no one knew it, and that the king's son was so distressed that he would give anything in the world to know who she was.

Cinderella smiled, and said she must have been beautiful indeed.

"Oh, how lucky you are. Could I not manage to see her? Oh, please, Javotte, lend me the yellow dress which you wear every day."

"Indeed!" said Javotte, "that is a fine idea. Lend my dress to a grubby cinder-clod like you – you must think me mad!"

Cinderella had expected this refusal. She was in no way upset, for she would have been very greatly embarrassed had her sister been willing to lend her the dress.

The next day the two sisters went to the ball, and so did Cinderella, even more splendidly attired than the first time.

The king's son was always at her elbow, and paid her endless compliments.

The young girl enjoyed herself so much that she forgot her godmother's bidding completely, and when the first stroke of midnight fell upon her ears, she thought it was no more than eleven o'clock.

She rose and fled as nimbly as a fawn. The prince followed her, but could not catch her. She let fall one of her glass slippers, however, and this the prince picked up with tender care.

When Cinderella reached home she was out of breath, without coach, without lackeys, and in her shabby clothes. Nothing remained of all her splendid clothes save one of the little slippers, the fellow to the one which she had let fall.

Inquiries were made of the palace doorkeepers as to whether they had seen a princess go out, but they declared they had seen no one leave except a young girl, very ill-clad, who looked more like a peasant than a young lady.

When her two sisters returned from the ball, Cinderella asked them if they had again enjoyed themselves, and if the beautiful lady had been there. They told her that she was present, but had fled away when midnight sounded, and in such haste that she had let fall one of her little glass slippers, the prettiest thing in the world. They added that the king's son, who picked it up, had done nothing but gaze at it for the rest of the ball, from which it was plain that he was deeply in love with its beautiful owner.

They spoke the truth. A few days later, the king's son caused a proclamation to be made by trumpeters, that he would take for wife the owner of the foot which the slipper would fit.

They tried it first on the princesses, then on the duchesses and the whole of the Court, but in vain. Presently they brought it to the home of the two sisters, who did all they could to squeeze a foot into the slipper. This, however, they could not manage.

Cinderella was looking on and recognised her slipper: "Let me see," she cried, laughingly, "if it will not fit me."

Her sisters burst out laughing, and began to gibe at her, but the equerry who was trying on the slipper looked closely at Cinderella. Observing that she was very beautiful he declared that the claim was quite a fair one, and that his orders were to try the slipper on every maiden. He bade Cinderella sit down, and on putting the slipper to her little foot he perceived that the latter slid in without trouble, and was moulded to its shape like wax.

Great was the astonishment of the two sisters at this, and greater still when Cinderella drew from her pocket the other little slipper. This she likewise drew on.

At that very moment her godmother appeared on the scene. She gave a tap with her wand to Cinderella's clothes, and transformed them into a dress even more magnificent than her previous ones.

The two sisters recognised her for the beautiful person whom they had seen at the ball, and threw themselves at her feet, begging her pardon for all the ill-treatment she had suffered at their hands.

Cinderella raised them, and declaring as she embraced them that she pardoned them with all her heart, bade them to love her well in future.

She was taken to the palace of the young prince in all her new array. He found her more beautiful than ever, and was married to her a few days afterwards.

Cinderella was as good as she was beautiful. She set aside apartments in the palace for her two sisters, and married them the very same day to two gentlemen of high rank about the Court.

MORAL

Beauty in a maid is an extraordinary treasure;
One never tires of admiring it.
But what we mean by graciousness
Is beyond price and still more precious.
It was this which her godmother gave Cinderella,
Teaching her to become a Queen.
(So the moral of this story goes.)
Lasses, this is a better gift than looks so fair
For winning over a heart successfully.
Graciousness is the true gift of the Fairies.
Without it, one can do nothing;
With it, one can do all!

ANOTHER MORAL

It is surely a great advantage
To have spirit and courage,
Good breeding and common sense,
And other qualities of this sort,
Which are the gifts of Heaven!
You will do well to own these;
But for success, they may well be in vain
If, as a final gift, one has not
The blessing of godfather or godmother.

Little Red Riding Hood

ONCE UPON A TIME there was a little village girl, the prettiest that had ever been seen. Her mother doted on her. Her grandmother was even fonder, and made her a little red hood, which became her so well that eve where she went by the name of Little Red Riding Hood.

One day her mother, who had just made and baked some cakes, said to her:

"Go and see how your grandmother is, for I have been told that she is ill. Take her a cake and this little pot of butter."

Little Red Riding Hood set off at once for the house of her grandmother, who lived in another village.

On her way through a wood she met old Father Wolf. He would have very much liked to eat her, but dared not do so on account of some wood-cutters who were in the forest. He asked her where she was going. The poor child, not knowing that it was dangerous to stop and listen to a wolf, said:

"I am going to see my grandmother, and am taking

her a cake and a pot of butter which my mother has sent to her."

"Does she live far away?" asked the Wolf.

"Oh, yes," replied Little Red Riding Hood; "it is yonder by the mill which you can see right below there, and it is the first house in the village."

"Well now," said the Wolf, "I think I shall go and see her too. I will go by this path, and you by that path, and we will see who gets there first."

The Wolf set off running with all his might by the shorter road, and the little girl continued on her way by the longer road. As she went she amused herself by gathering nuts, running after the butterflies, and making nosegays of the wild flowers which she found.

The Wolf was not long in reaching the grandmother's house.

He knocked. Toc Toc.

"Who is there?"

"It is your granddaughter, Red Riding Hood," said the Wolf, disguising his voice, "and I bring you a cake and a little pot of butter as a present from my mother."

The worthy grandmother was in bed, not being very well, and cried out to him:

"Pull out the peg and the latch will fall."

The Wolf drew out the peg and the door flew open. Then he sprang upon the poor old lady and ate her up in less than no time, for he had been more than three days without food.

After that he shut the door, lay down in the grandmother's

bed, and waited for Little Riding Hood.

Presently she came and knocked. Toc Toc.

"Who is there?"

Now Little Red Riding Hood on hearing the Wolf's gruff voice was at first frightened, but thinking that her grandmother had a bad cold, she replied:

"It is your granddaughter, Red Riding Hood, and I bring you a cake and a little pot of butter from my mother."

Softening his voice, the Wolf called out to her:

"Pull out the peg and the latch will fall."

Little Red Riding Hood drew out the peg and the door flew open.

When he saw her enter, the Wolf hid himself in the bed beneath the counterpane.

"Put the cake and the little pot of butter on the bin," he said, "and come up on the bed with me."

Little Red Riding Hood took off her cloak, but when she climbed up on the bed she was astonished to see how her grandmother looked in her nightgown.

"Grandmother dear!" she exclaimed, "what big arms you have!"

"The better to embrace you, my child!"

"Grandmother dear, what big legs you have!"

"The better to run with, my child!"

"Grandmother dear, what big ears you have!"

"The better to hear with, my child!"

"Grandmother dear, what big eyes you have!"

"The better to see with, my child!"

"Grandmother dear, what big teeth you have!"
"The better to eat you with!"
With these words the wicked Wolf leapt upon Little
Red Riding Hood and gobbled her up.

MORAL

From this story one learns that children,
Especially young lasses,
Pretty, courteous and well-bred,
Do very wrong to listen to strangers,
And it is not an unheard thing
If the Wolf is thereby provided with his dinner.
I say Wolf, for all wolves
Are not of the same sort;
There is one kind with an amenable disposition
Neither noisy, nor hateful, nor angry,
But tame, obliging and gentle,
Following the young maids
In the streets, even into their homes.
Alas! who does not know that these gentle wolves
Are of all such creatures the most dangerous!

Blue Beard

ONCE UPON A TIME there was a man who owned splendid town and country houses, gold and silver plate, tapestries and coaches gilt all over. But the poor fellow had a blue beard, and this made him so ugly and frightful that there was not a woman or girl who did not run away at sight of him.

Amongst his neighbours was a lady of high degree who had two surpassingly beautiful daughters. He asked for the hand of one of these in marriage, leaving it to their mother to choose which should be bestowed upon him. Both girls, however, raised objections, and his offer was bandied from one to the other, neither being able to bring herself to accept a man with a blue beard. Another reason for their distaste was the fact that he had already married several wives, and no one knew what had become of them.

In order that they might become better acquainted, Blue Beard invited the two girls, with their mother and three or four of their best friends, to meet a party of young men from the neighbourhood at one of his country houses. Here they spent eight whole days, and throughout their stay there was a constant round of picnics, hunting and fishing expeditions, dances, dinners, and luncheons; and they never slept at all, through spending all the night in playing merry pranks upon each other. In short, everything went so gaily that the younger daughter began to think the master of the house had not so very blue a beard after all, and that he was an exceedingly agreeable man. As soon as the party returned to town their marriage took place.

At the end of a month Blue Beard informed his wife that important business obliged him to make a journey into a distant part of the country, which would occupy at least six weeks. He begged her to amuse herself well during his absence, and suggested that she should invite some of her friends and take them, if she liked, to the country. He was particularly anxious that she should enjoy herself thoroughly.

"Here," he said, "are the keys of the two large store-rooms, and here is the one that locks up the gold and silver plate which is not in everyday use. This key belongs to the strong-boxes where my gold and silver is kept, this to the caskets containing my jewels; while here you have the master-key which gives admittance to all the apartments. As regards this little key, it is the key of the small room at the end of the long passage on the lower floor. You may open everything, you may go everywhere, but I forbid you to enter this little room. And I forbid you so seriously that if you were indeed to open the door, I should be so angry that I might do anything."

She promised to follow out these instructions exactly, and after embracing her, Blue Beard steps into his coach and is off upon his journey.

Her neighbours and friends did not wait to be invited before coming to call upon the young bride, so great was their eagerness to see the splendours of her house. They had not dared to venture while her husband was there, for his blue beard frightened them. But in less than no time there they were, running in and out of the rooms, the closets, and the wardrobes, each of which was finer than the last. Presently they went upstairs to the storerooms, and there they could not admire enough the profusion and magnificence of the tapestries, beds, sofas, cabinets, tables, and stands. There were mirrors in which they could view themselves from top to toe, some with frames of plate glass, others with frames of silver and gilt lacquer, that were the most superb and beautiful things that had ever been seen. They were loud and persistent in their envy of their friend's good fortune. She, on the other hand, derived little amusement from the sight of all these riches, the reason being that she was impatient to go and inspect the little room on the lower floor.

So overcome with curiosity was she that, without reflecting upon the discourtesy of leaving her guests, she ran down a private staircase, so precipitately that twice or thrice she nearly broke her neck, and so reached the door of the little room. There she paused for a while, thinking of the prohibition which her husband had made, and reflecting that harm might come to her as a result of disobedience. But the temptation was so great that she could not conquer it. Taking the little key, with a trembling hand she opened the door of the room.

At first she saw nothing, for the windows were closed, but after a few moments she perceived dimly that the floor was entirely covered with clotted blood, and that in this were reflected the dead bodies of several women that hung along the walls. These were all the wives of Blue Beard, whose throats he had cut, one after another.

She thought to die of terror, and the key of the room, which she had just withdrawn from the lock, fell from her hand.

When she had somewhat regained her senses, she picked up the key, closed the door, and went up to her chamber to compose herself a little. But this she could not do, for her nerves were too shaken. Noticing that the key of the little room was stained with blood, she wiped it two or three times. But the blood did not go. She washed it well, and even rubbed it with sand and grit. Always the blood remained. For the key was bewitched, and there was no means of cleaning it completely. When the blood was removed from one side, it reappeared on the other.

Blue Beard returned from his journey that very evening. He had received some letters on the way, he said, from which he learned that the business upon which he had set forth had just been concluded to his satisfaction. His wife did everything she could to make it appear that she was delighted by his speedy return.

On the morrow he demanded the keys. She gave them to him, but with so trembling a hand that he guessed at once what had happened.

"How comes it," he said to her, "that the key of the little room is not with the others?"

"I must have left it upstairs upon my table," she said.

"Do not fail to bring it to me presently," said Blue Beard.

After several delays the key had to be brought. Blue Beard examined it and addressed his wife.

"Why is there blood on this key?"

"I do not know at all," replied the poor woman, paler than death.

"You do not know at all?" exclaimed Blue Beard; "I know well enough. You wanted to enter the little room! Well, madam, enter it you shall – you shall go and take your place among the ladies you have seen there."

She threw herself at her husband's feet, asking his pardon with tears, and with all the signs of a true repentance for her disobedience. She would have softened a rock, in her beauty and distress, but Blue Beard had a heart harder than any stone.

"You must die, madam," he said; "and at once."

"Since I must die," she replied, gazing at him with eyes that were wet with tears, "give me a little time to say my prayers."

"I give you one quarter of an hour," replied Blue Beard, "but not a moment longer."

When the poor girl was alone, she called her sister to her and said:

"Sister Anne" – for that was her name – "go up, I implore you, to the top of the tower, and see if my brothers are not approaching. They promised that they would come and visit me to-day. If you see them, make signs to them to hasten."

Sister Anne went up to the top of the tower, and the poor unhappy girl cried out to her from time to time:

"Anne, Sister Anne, do you see nothing coming?"

And Sister Anne replied:

"I see nought but dust in the sun and the green grass growing."

Presently Blue Beard, grasping a great cutlass, cried out at the top of his voice:

"Come down quickly, or I shall come upstairs myself."

"Oh please, one moment more," called out his wife.

And at the same moment she cried in a whisper:

"Anne, Sister Anne, do you see nothing coming?"

"I see nought but dust in the sun and the green grass growing."

"Come down at once, I say," shouted Blue Beard, "or I will come upstairs myself."

"I am coming," replied his wife.

Then she called:

"Anne, Sister Anne, do you see nothing coming?"

"I see," replied Sister Anne, "a great cloud of dust which comes this way."

"Is it my brothers?"

"Alas, sister, no; it is but a flock of sheep."

"Do you refuse to come down?" roared Blue Beard.

"One little moment more," exclaimed his wife.

Once more she cried:

"Anne, Sister Anne, do you see nothing coming?"

"I see," replied her sister, "two horsemen who come this way, but they are as yet a long way off – Heaven be praised," she exclaimed a moment later, "they are my brothers – I am signalling to them all I can to hasten."

Blue Beard let forth so mighty a shout that the whole house shook. The poor wife went down and cast herself at his feet, all dishevelled and in tears.

"That avails you nothing," said Blue Beard; "you must die."

Seizing her by the hair with one hand, and with the other brandishing the cutlass aloft, he made as if to cut off her head.

The poor woman, turning towards him and fixing a dying gaze upon him, begged for a brief moment in which to collect her thoughts.

"No! no!" he cried; "commend your soul to Heaven." And raising his arm –

At this very moment there came so loud a knocking at the gate that Blue Beard stopped short. The gate was opened, and two horsemen dashed in, who drew their swords and rode straight at Blue Beard. The latter recognised them as the brothers of his wife – one of them a dragoon, and the other a musketeer – and fled instantly in an effort to escape. But the two brothers were so close upon him that they caught him ere he could gain the first flight of steps. They plunged their swords through his body and left him dead. The poor woman was nearly as dead as her husband, and had not the strength to rise and embrace her brothers.

It was found that Blue Beard had no heirs, and that consequently his wife became mistress of all his wealth. She devoted a portion to arranging a marriage between her Sister Anne and a young gentleman with whom the latter had been for some time in love, while another portion purchased a captain's commission for each of her brothers. The rest formed a dowry for her own marriage with a very worthy man, who banished from her mind all memory of the evil days she had spent with Blue Beard.

MORAL

Curiosity, in spite of its great charms,
Often brings with it serious regrets.
Every day a thousand examples appear.
In spite of a maiden's wishes, it's a fruitless pleasure,
For once satisfied, curiosity offers nothing,
And ever does it cost more dearly.

continued –

ANOTHER MORAL

If one takes a sensible point of view
And studies this grim story,
He will recognize that this tale
Is one of days long past.
No longer is the husband so terrifying,
Demanding the impossible,
Being both dissatisfied and jealous;
In the presence of his wife he now
is gracious enough,
And no matter what colour his beard may be
One does not have to guess who is master!

The Ridiculous Wishes

HERE WAS ONCE a poor wood-cutter who, tired of his hard life, longed for rest in the world to come. In his unhappiness, he declared that in all his days Heaven had not granted even one of his wishes.

One day in the woods, as the wood-cutter was complaining of his unhappy lot, Jupiter appeared before him, his thunderbolts in his hands. It would be difficult to picture the terror of the poor man.

"I desire nothing," he said, casting himself on the ground. "I will give up my wishes if you, in turn, will give up your thunder. That's a fair exchange!"

"Have no fear," said Jupiter. "I have heard your complaints and I have come to show you how unfairly you judge me. Now listen! I am King of all the world and I promise to grant your first three wishes, no matter what they may be. See that they make you happy and content; and since your happiness depends on them, think carefully before you make them."

With these words, Jupiter returned to his heavens

and the happy wood-cutter, taking up his bundle of sticks, hurried to his home. Never had his burden seemed so light.

"This is an important matter," he said to himself. "I certainly must have my wife's advice.

"Hey, Fanchon," he shouted, as he entered his cottage. "Let us make up a good fire. We are rich for the rest of our lives. All we have to do is to make three wishes!"

With this, he told his wife what had happened, whereupon she in her imagination began to form a thousand plans. But realizing the importance of acting prudently, she said to her husband, "Blaise, my dear, let us not spoil anything by our impatience. We must think things over very carefully. Let us put off our first wish until tomorrow. Let us sleep on it."

"I think you are right," said he. "But first go draw some of that special wine."

On her return, the wood-cutter drank deeply and leaned back in his chair before the fire. "To match such a fine blaze," he said, "I wish we had a measure of sausage. It would go very well indeed!"

Scarcely had he spoken these words when his wife, to her great astonishment, saw a long link of sausage moving over to them like a snake from the chimney corner. She cried out in alarm, but realizing at once that this was the result of the wish which her foolish husband had made, she began to abuse and scold him angrily.

"When you might," she said, "have a kingdom, with gold, pearls, rubies, diamonds, fine clothes – and all you wish for is a sausage!"

"Alas," her husband replied. "I was wrong. I made a very bad choice. I admit my mistake. Next time I will do better."

"Yes! Yes!" said his wife. "I'll repeat it till Doomsday. To make such a choice as you did, you must be a donkey."

At this the husband became very angry and almost wished his wife was dead. "Mankind," he said, "is born to suffer. A curse on this and all sausages. I wish that it was hanging from the end of your nose!"

The wish was heard at once in Heaven, and the sausage fastened itself on her nose. Fanchon had once been pretty and, to tell the truth, this ornament did not have a very pleasing effect. Since it hung down over her face, however, it interfered with her talking, and this was such an advantage to her husband that he did not think he had wished too badly.

"With my remaining wish I could very well still make myself a king," he said to himself. "But we must think of the queen, too, and her unhappiness if she were to sit on the throne with her new yard-long nose. She must decide which she wants, to be a queen with that nose or a wood-cutter's wife and an ordinary person."

Whereupon his wife agreed that they had no choice. She would never have the riches and diamonds and fine clothes she had dreamed of, but she would be herself again if the last wish would free her from the frightful sausage on her nose.

And so the wood-cutter did not change his lot. He did not become a king. His purse was not filled with gold. He was only too glad to use his remaining wish in restoring his poor wife to her former state.

Donkey-Skin

ONCE UPON A TIME there was a King who was the most powerful ruler in the whole world. Kind and just in peace and terrifying in war, his enemies feared him while his subjects were happy and content. His wife and faithful companion was both charming and beautiful. From their union a daughter had been born.

Their large and magnificent palace was filled with courtiers, and their stables boasted steeds large and small, of every description. But what surprised everyone on entering these stables was that the place of honour was held by a donkey with two big ears.

Now Heaven, which seems to mingle good with evil, suddenly permitted a bitter illness to attack the Queen. Help was sought on all sides, but neither the learned physicians nor the charlatans were able to arrest the fever which increased daily. Finally, her last hour having come, the Queen said to her husband: "Promise me that if, when I am gone, you find a woman wiser and more beautiful than I, you will marry her and so provide an heir for your throne." Since he believed it would be impossible to find such a woman, the King agreed and shortly thereafter his wife died in his arms.

For a time the King was inconsolable in his grief, both day and night. Some months later, however, on the urging of his courtiers, he agreed to marry again, but this was not an easy matter, for he had to keep his promise to his wife and search as he might, he could not find a new wife with all the attractions he sought. Only his daughter had a charm and beauty which even the Queen had not possessed.

The King, still grieving deeply for his wife, became confused in his mind and, imagining that he was still a young man, he thought his daughter was the maiden he had once wooed to be his wife. His daughter, however, became sad and frightened and tried to show her father the mistake he was making. Deeply troubled at this turn of events, she sought out her fairy godmother who lived in a grotto of coral and pearls.

"I know why you have come here," her godmother said. "In your heart there is a great sadness. But I am here to help you and nothing can harm you if you follow my advice. You must not disobey your father, but first tell him that you must have a dress which has the colour of the Sky. Certainly he will never be able to meet that request."

And so the young Princess went all trembling to her father. But he, the moment he heard her request, summoned his best tailors and ordered them, without delay, to make a dress the colour of the Sky – or they could be assured he would hang them all.

The following day the dress was shown to the Princess. It was the most beautiful blue of Heaven. Filled now with both happiness and fear, she did not know what to do, but her godmother again told her: "Ask for a dress the colour of the Moon. Surely your father will not be able to give you this."

No sooner had the Princess made the request than the King summoned his embroiderers and ordered that a dress the colour of the Moon be completed by the fourth day. On that very day it was ready and the Princess was again delighted with its beauty. But still her godmother urged her once again to make a request of the King, this time for a dress as bright and shining as the Sun. This time the King summoned a wealthy jeweller and ordered him to make a cloth of gold and diamonds, warning him that if he failed he would die. Within a week the jeweller had finished the dress, so beautiful and radiant that it dazzled the eyes of everyone who saw it.

The Princess did not know how to thank the King, but once again her godmother whispered in her ear. "Ask him for the skin of the donkey in the royal stable. The King will not consider your request seriously. You will not receive it or I am badly mistaken." But she did not understand how extraordinary was the King's desire to please his daughter. Almost immediately the donkey's skin was brought to the Princess.

Once again she was frightened and once again her godmother came to her assistance. "Pretend," she said, "to give in to the King. Promise him anything he wishes, but, at the same time, prepare to escape to some far country.

"Here," she continued, "is a chest in which we will put your clothes, your mirror, the things for your toilet, your diamonds and other jewels. I will give you my magic wand. Whenever you have it in your hand, the chest will follow you everywhere, always hidden underground. Whenever you wish to open the chest, as soon as you touch the wand to the ground, the chest will appear.

"To conceal you, the donkey's skin will be an admirable disguise, for when you are inside it, no one will believe that anyone so beautiful could be hidden in anything so frightful."

Early in the morning the Princess disappeared as she was advised. They searched everywhere for her, in houses, along the roads, wherever she might have been, but in vain. No one could imagine what had become of her.

The Princess, meanwhile, was continuing her flight. To everyone she met, she extended her hands, begging them to find her some place where she might find work. But she looked so unattractive and indeed so repulsive in her donkey-skin disguise that no one would have anything to do with such a creature.

Farther and still farther she journeyed until finally she

came to a farm where they needed a poor wretch to wash the dishcloths and clean out the pig troughs. They also made her work in a corner of the kitchen where she was exposed to the low jokes and ridicule of all the other servants.

On Sundays she had a little rest for, having completed her morning tasks, she went to her room and closed the door and bathed. Then she opened the chest, took out her toilet jars and set them up, with the mirror, before her. Having made herself beautiful once more, she tried on her Moon dress, then that one which shone like the Sun and, finally, the lovely blue dress. Her only regret was that she did not have room enough to display their trains. She was happy, however, in seeing herself young again, and this pleasure carried her along from one Sunday to the next.

On this great farm where she worked there was an aviary belonging to a powerful King. All sorts of unusual birds with strange habits were kept there. The King's son often stopped at this farm on his return from the hunt in order to rest and enjoy a cool drink with his courriers.

From a distance Donkey-Skin gazed on him with tenderness and remembered that beneath her dirt and rags she still had the heart of a Princess. What a grand manner he has, she thought. How gracious he is! How happy must she be to whom his heart is pledged! If he should give me a dress of only the simplest sort, I would feel more splendid wearing it than any of these which I have.

One day the young Prince, seeking adventure from court yard to court yard, came to the obscure hallway where Donkey-Skin had her humble room. By chance he put his eye to the key hole. It was a feast-day and Donkey-Skin had put on her dress of gold and diamonds which shone as brightly as the Sun. The Prince was breathless at her beauty, her youthfulness, and her modesty. Three times he was on the point of entering her room, but each time refrained.

On his return to his father's palace, the Prince became very thoughtful, sighing day and night and refusing to attend any of the balls and carnivals. He lost his appetite and finally sank into a sad and deadly melancholy. He asked who this beautiful maiden was that lived in such squalor and was told that it was Donkey-Skin, the ugliest animal one could find, except the wolf, and a certain cure for love. This he would not believe and he refused to forget what he had seen.

His mother, the Queen, begged him to tell her what was wrong. Instead, he moaned, wept and sighed. He would say nothing, except that he wanted Donkey-Skin to make him a cake with her own hands.

O Heavens, they told her, this Donkey-Skin is only a poor, drab servant. "It makes no difference," replied the Queen. "We must do as he says. It is the only way to save him."

So Donkey-Skin took some flour which she had ground especially fine, and some salt, some butter and some fresh eggs and shut herself alone in her room to make the cake. But first she washed her face and hands and put on a silver smock in honour of the task she had undertaken.

Now the story goes that, working perhaps a little too hastily, there fell from Donkey-Skin's finger into the batter a ring of great value. Some who know the outcome of this story think that she may have dropped the ring on purpose, and they are probably right, for when the Prince stopped at her door and looked through the key hole, she must have known it. And she was sure that the ring would be received most joyfully by her lover.

The Prince found the cake so good that in his ravishing hunger, he almost swallowed the ring! When he saw the beautiful emerald and the band of gold that traced the shape of Donkey-Skin's finger, his heart was filled with an indescribable joy. At once he put the ring under his pillow, but his illness increased daily until finally the doctors, seeing him grow worse, gravely concluded that he was sick with love.

Marriage, whatever may be said against it, is an excellent remedy for love sickness. And so it was decided that the Prince was to marry. "But I insist," he said, "that I will wed only the person whom this ring fits." This unusual demand surprised the King and Queen very much, but the Prince was so ill that they did not dare object.

A search began for whoever might be able to fit the

ring on her finger, no matter what the station in life. It was rumored throughout the land that in order to win the Prince one must have a very slender finger. Every charlatan had his secret method of making the finger slim. One suggested scraping it as though it was a turnip. Another recommended cutting away a small piece. Still another, with a certain liquid, planned to decrease the size by removing the skin.

At last the trials began with the Princesses, the Marquesses and the Duchesses, but their fingers, although delicate, were too big for the ring. Then the Countesses, the Baronesses and all the Nobility presented their hands, but all in vain. Next came the working girls, who often have slender and beautiful fingers, but the ring would not fit them, either.

Finally it was necessary to turn to the servants, the kitchen help, the slaveys and the poultry keepers, with their red and dirty hands. Putting the tiny ring on their clumsy fingers was like trying to thread a big rope through the eye of a needle.

At last the trials were finished. There remained only Donkey-Skin in her far corner of the farm kitchen. Who could dream that she ever would be Queen?

"And why not?" asked the Prince. "Ask her to come here." At that, some started to laugh; others cried out against bringing that frightful creature into the room. But when she drew out from under the donkey skin a little hand as white as ivory and the ring was placed on her finger and fitted perfectly, everyone was astounded.

They prepared to take her to the King at once, but she asked that before she appeared before her lord and master, she be permitted to change her clothes. To tell the truth, there was some smiling at this request, but when she arrived at the palace in her beautiful dress, the richness of which had never been equalled, with her blonde hair all alight with diamonds and her blue eyes sweet and appealing and even her waist so slender that two hands could have encircled it, then even the gracious ladies of the court seemed, by comparison, to have lost all their charms. In all this happiness and excitement, the King did not fail to notice the charms of his prospective daughter-in-law and the Queen was completely delighted with her. The Prince himself found his happiness almost more than he could bear. Preparations for the wedding were begun at once, and the Kings of all the surrounding countries were invited. Some came from the East, mounted on huge elephants. Others were so fierce-looking that they frightened the little children. From all the corners of the world they came and descended on the court in great numbers.

But neither the Prince nor the many visiting Kings appeared in such splendour as the bride's father, who now recognized his daughter and begged her forgiveness.

"How kind Heaven is," he said, "to let me see you again, my dear daughter." Weeping with joy, he embraced her tenderly. His happiness was shared by all and the future husband was delighted to find that his father-in-law was such a powerful King. At that moment the fairy godmother arrived, too, and told the whole story of what had happened, and what she had to tell added the final triumph for Donkey-Skin.

It is not hard to see that the moral of this tale is that it is better to undergo the greatest hardships rather than to fail in one's duty, that virtue may sometimes seem ill-fated but will always triumph in the end.

MORAL

The story of Donkey-Skin may be hard to believe, but so long as there are children, mothers and grandmothers in this world, it will be fondly remembered by all.

Patient Griselda

T THE FOOT of the mountains where the Po escapes from its bed of reeds to the neighbouring plain, there once lived a youthful and gallant Prince, the favourite of the whole countryside. Combining in himself all the gifts of body and spirit, he was strong, clever, skilful in war, and displayed great enthusiasm for the arts. He loved fighting and victory, too, along with all mighty endeavours and deeds of glory – everything which makes one's name live in history. But more than all these, his greatest pleasure lay in the happiness of his people.

This splendid disposition was obscured, however, by a sombre cloud, a melancholy mood which caused the Prince to feel, in the depths of his heart, that all women were faithless and deceivers. Even in a woman of the highest distinction he saw only the heart of a hypocrite, elated with pride. To him she was a cruel enemy whose unbroken ambition was to gain the mastery over whatever unhappy man might surrender to her.

Each day the Prince gave his morning to his royal business. He ruled wisely, doing everything he felt best for his people – the frail orphan, the oppressed widow, protecting the rights of all. The remainder of the day was devoted to the chase, either the stag or the bear. These, in spite of their ferocity, frightened him less than the charming women whom he shunned daily.

His subjects, nevertheless, kept urging him to provide them with an heir to the throne, someone who would rule them with the same affection that the Prince had always shown.

In reply to their urgings, the Prince said: "This zeal with which you urge me to marry pleases me greatly. I am deeply touched. But I am convinced," he added, "that happiness can be found in a marriage only when one of the two partners is dominant over the other. If, therefore, you wish to see me wed, find me a young beauty without pride or vanity, obedient, with tried and proved patience and, above all, without a domineering will of her own. Once you have found her, I will marry!"

The Prince, having finished these comments, flung himself on his horse and galloped off to join his hounds. Over field and meadow he flew, to find his fellow huntsmen waiting for him, ready and alert. Therefore, he ordered the chase to begin at once and urged the dogs after the stag. The blare of the horns, the thunder of the horses' hooves, and the baying of the hounds filled the forest with tumult so that the echoes were repeated endlessly, growing louder and louder in the hollows of the woods.

By chance, or perhaps by destiny, the Prince turned one day into a winding road where none of the huntsmen followed him. The further he went, the more widely he became separated from them, until finally he reached a point where he no longer heard either the hounds or the horns of the huntsmen.

The place where his strange adventure had led him, with its clear streams and shadowy trees, filled the Prince with awe. The simple and unspoiled nature about him was so beautiful and pure that a thousand times he blessed his wanderings from the well-known paths.

Filled with the reveries which pervaded the woods, fields and streams, his heart and eyes were suddenly confronted by a most delightful object, the sweetest and kindliest ever seen under heaven. It was a young shepherdess.

She would, indeed, have tamed the most savage heart. Her complexion was like a lily whose fresh whiteness had always been shielded from the sun. Her lips were most engaging. Her eyes, softened by dark lashes, were bluer than the sky and even more bright.

The Prince, transported with delight, slipped back quietly into the wood where he might gaze unseen on the beauty by which his heart was possessed. The noise which he made, however, caused the girl to glance in his direction. The moment she saw him she blushed deeply and this, in turn, added to her beauty. Under this innocent veil of modesty the Prince discovered a simplicity, a sweetness and a sincerity which he did not believe possible in any woman. He drew nearer to her, and even more timid and confused than she, he explained in a trembling voice that he had lost all trace of the other huntsmen and asked her if perchance the chase had passed through that part of the wood.

"No one has been seen in this solitary place except you," she said, "but do not be disturbed. I will put you on the right road again."

"For this extraordinary good fortune," said the Prince, "I cannot be thankful enough to Heaven. For a long time I have been accustomed to visit such places as these, but until today I have not realized how precious they might be to me."

As the maiden saw the Prince kneel on the edge of the stream to quench his thirst, she called to him to wait, and hurrying to her little cottage, she returned with a cup which she graciously handed him. All the precious goblets of crystal, agate and gold, sparkling and artfully designed, never had for him, in their silly uselessness, half the beauty of this clay cup which the shepherdess had just given him.

To find an easy road whereby the Prince might

return to his palace, together they journeyed through the woods, over steep rocks and across torrents and as he followed along this unfamiliar route, the Prince observed all the landmarks carefully. He was dreaming already that he would wish some day to return, and his love was making a faithful map for him to do so.

From a dark grove where finally the shepherdess had led him he spied through the branches the golden roofs of his magnificent palace. Separated shortly from the beautiful girl, he was soon beset by a deep grief. The recollection of his recent adventure filled him with pleasure, yet on the morrow he was depressed with weariness and sorrow.

As soon as he could, he arranged another hunt and cleverly giving his followers the slip, sought again the woods and hills where the young shepherdess dwelt. There he found her, living with her father, and learned that her name was Griselda. Together the girl and the old man lived simply on the milk of their flock and wove their garments from the fleece.

As the days went by, the more he saw of her, the brighter the Prince's love burned for the shepherdess. He was filled with an extreme happiness and, finally, one day he called his counsellors together and spoke to them:

"In accordance with your wishes, I am at last planning to wed, although I shall not take a wife from a strange land but from someone among us – someone lovely, wise and well-bred. I shall eagerly await the great moment to inform you of my choice."

When this news was released, it was carried every-where and no one could measure the joy with which it was received on every side.

It was amusing to see the useless trouble to which the belles of the town went to win the approval of their Prince for whom modesty and simplicity had a charm above all else, as he had told them a hundred times. They changed their manners and their dress; they lowered their voices; they even coughed in a pious tone; they reduced their hairdos a half foot; they covered their necks and lengthened their sleeves, so that one scarcely saw the ends of their fingers.

The workmen and artists of the town laboured diligently for the wedding day which they knew was approaching. Magnificent floats were contrived in an entirely new style in which gold which was used lavishly was the least of their ornaments. Here, on one side, grandstands were set up from which the pomp and ceremony might better be seen. There, in another direction, great arches were erected, celebrating the glories of their warrior Prince and the brilliant victory of Love over him.

Here were forges of the industrial arts whose fires, with harmless thundering, frightened the Earth, their sparks like a thousand new stars adorning the heavens.

There a clever ballet was devised, with merry foolishness, and there, too, in an opera lovelier than any which had ever been produced in Italy, were heard a thousand melodious songs.

At last the famous wedding day arrived! The very heavens mingled the crimson of the dawn with their gold and blue as the lovely maidens of the land wakened from their slumbers. Sightseers arrived from all directions. In many places guards were posted to hold the crowds in check. The palace echoed with the sounds of horns, flutes, oboes and rustic bagpipes, while on every side could be heard the drums and trumpets.

At last the Prince came out from his palace, surrounded by his courtiers. A great cry of joy arose, but a moment later everyone was amazed when, at the first turn of the road, he took the path into the nearby forest, just as he had done many times before. "There," everyone mistakenly said, "is where his interest lies. In spite of his love, the hunt holds the first place in his heart."

The Prince quickly crossed the open farm lands and, reaching the hills, entered the woods, to the astonishment of the troop of courtiers who accompanied him.

After having passed along several by-paths which his heart with happiness remembered, he found himself at the rustic cottage where his precious loved one lived.

Griselda had heard, too, about the wedding and, dressed in her best, was waiting outside her little house, before going to see the celebration.

"Where are you going so gaily and in such haste?" asked the Prince, drawing near and gazing on her tenderly. "Stop hurrying, my dear shepherdess. The wedding for which you are so ready to leave here and in which I am to become a husband will never take place without you as part of it. Yes, I love you and I have chosen you from among a thousand young beauties to spend the rest of my life with, if, of course, my hopes are not disappointed."

"My lord," she replied, "I could never dare believe that I might be destined for such an honour. Are you seeking to make sport with me?"

"Not for a moment," the Prince answered. "I am most sincere. But before we pledge an eternal vow between us it will be necessary for you to swear that you will never have any other wishes than what I shall desire."

"I swear it," she said, "and give you my promise. If I were to marry the least important man in the world, I should agree to obey him. His yoke would be a gentle one for me. How much rather, then, would I obey you if I found you my lord and master."

So the prince had spoken and while the court applauded his choice, he asked the shepherdess please to be patient as she was instructed in those graces and deportment which should belong to the bride of a king. Those whose duty it was displayed all their skill in making these adjustments for her.

Whereupon there slipped from the little cottage,

stately and radiant, the charming shepherdess. Not only was there applause everywhere for her beauty, but beyond this for her real ornament, an innocent simplicity.

In a magnificent coach of gold and ivory, which had followed the course of the Prince, the shepherdess was seated in full majesty, and the Prince, proudly there with her, found no less glory in his role of a lover than when marching in triumph following a great victory. The courtiers followed them as they moved gaily toward the palace.

Meanwhile the whole town impatiently awaited the Prince's return. Suddenly he appeared and they rushed to meet him. Surrounded by a great crowd of people, the wedding coach could scarcely move. At the shouts of joy, doubled and re-doubled, the horses were frightened. They reared, stamped their hooves, dashed forward and then drew back again further than they had advanced. But at long last they reached the church and with solemn vows the two lovers were united in marriage.

When they finally reached the palace, a thousand diversions awaited them. Dancing, games, racing and tournaments spread merriment throughout the city. And the love of the Prince and the shepherdess was like a crowning glory of the day!

On the next day, the various sections of the country joined in congratulating the Prince and Princess in speeches by their leaders. Surrounded by her ladies-

in-waiting, Griselda, without showing any surprise,
listened to them like a princess and like a princess she
replied. In everything she did, she acted so wisely
that it seemed as though Heaven had given her its
richest blessings of the mind as well as of the body.
She easily accustomed herself to the ways of the new
world about her and was quickly as much at home
there in the court as she had been formerly in taking
care of her sheep.

Before a year had passed their marriage was blessed
with a child, not a prince as might have been desired
but a little princess, so lovely and endearing that
every moment her father kept coming back to gaze
on her again. Her mother, still more enraptured,
never took her eyes off her. She even determined to
nurse the infant herself, for "how can I refuse her,"
she said, "when her cries insist on having me? Can I
be only a part mother of the child I love so much?"

In time the love of the Prince became a little less
ardent than formerly, so that his evil mood seemed to
grow again. It was as though a thick fog had obscured
his senses and corrupted his heart. In everything that
the Princess did he imagined that he saw little real
sincerity. Her outstanding goodness offended him; it
was a snare, he thought, for his credulity. His unhappy state of mind led him to believe every suspicion.
As a result of the melancholy with which his mind
had been tainted, he followed her about, watching
her. He seemed to enjoy limiting her pleasures and

alarming her, mixing the false with the true.

"I must not be lulled asleep," he said. "If these virtues of hers are indeed genuine, then even my most unreasonable actions will only strengthen them."

And so she was confined to the palace and retired to her rooms, far from the pleasures of the court. Convinced that one's wardrobe and its accessories are the dearest delight of a woman, the Prince rudely demanded her pearls, rubies, rings and jewels, all of which he had given her as a token of his affection when he became her husband.

She whose life was stainless, who had never been punished in any way, who had performed her every duty well, had been happy in giving as she had been in receiving:

"My husband plagues me only to test my love," she said, "and he only makes me suffer to arouse my sleeping virtues which might have perished in a long and peaceful repose. Let us be happy, then, in this harsh but worthwhile severity. For one is often happy only as one suffers."

The Prince was chagrined to see her obey freely all of his strictest orders. "I see," he said, "what lies behind this false goodness of hers and makes all my efforts useless. My blows have been directed only where there is no longer any love. But for her infant child, for the little princess, she has shown the greatest tenderness. If I am to succeed in my testing her, it is there that I must direct my efforts."

At the moment she was about to nurse the baby who was lying against her heart, smiling.

"I see that you love her," said the Prince. "It will be necessary, however, that while she is still very young I separate her from you so that she will be brought up with the right manners and will be protected from the bad habits into which she will surely fall if she remains with you. By the best of good luck I have found a lady who will bring her up with all the virtues and good manners which a princess should have. You will arrange, then, to part with her. They will be coming soon to take her away."

At these words, he left her, not having the courage to watch them snatch from her arms this pledge of their love. A thousand tears bathed her face as she watched in mournful dejection the darkest moment of her unhappiness.

As soon as those who were to carry out this cruel and sad undertaking appeared, she told them, "I must obey." Then, taking up her child, she gazed on her and kissing her with a mother's love, weeping, she gave her up. Alas, how bitter was her sorrow. To tear an infant from its mother's heart, this is Grief itself.

Not far from the city was a convent, famous for its antiquity, where the nuns lived according to strict rules under the eyes of an abbess, renowned for her piety. It was here in silence and without revealing the secret of her birth that they took the infant.

The Prince tried to escape, by hunting, from the

sharp remorse which embarrassed him over his extreme show of cruelty. He hesitated to visit the Princess, as one might fear to meet again a fierce tigress from whom its cub had been taken. Nevertheless, he was received tenderly by his wife and with the same affection which she had formerly shown during their happiest days.

At this remarkable and unexpected courage, he was touched with regret and shame but the strange mood that had come over him was still strong. And so, two days later, with affected tears, in order to deliver the final and supreme blow, he came to her to announce the death of the amiable child.

This unexpected blow wounded her deeply. Nevertheless, in spite of her sadness, having noticed how her husband seemed changed in appearance, she forgot her own grief and exerted every effort to console him in his false sorrow.

This goodness, this unique marvel of love, suddenly softened the Prince's harshness. It changed his heart so that he was inclined to announce that their child still lived. But his bitterness of spirit was still strong and fiercely upheld him in not revealing the mystery which it was so useless to conceal.

And so for fifteen years the sun moved through the various stages along its orbit and brought the changing seasons. Meanwhile the little princess in the convent grew in wisdom and stature. To the sweetness and simplicity which she inherited from her mother she added her father's pleasing and proud dignity, a combination which gave her a rare beauty of character. She shone like a bright star and, by chance, one of the noblemen at the court, young, well-bred and gallant, having glimpsed her through the gate of the convent, fell in love with her.

By that instinct which Nature has given the fairer sex of noticing the invisible wounds which their eyes make, at the moment they are made, the princess knew that she had found a tender lover. And having resisted for a little, as one has a right to do before giving in, she, for her part, fell completely in love, too.

Nothing was lacking in this young lover. He was handsome, courageous and came from an illustrious family. For a long time now the Prince had been observing him. And so it was with great joy that he learned that the two young people were in love. But he took a strange satisfaction in making them win the supreme happiness of their lives only by a series of vexations and torments. He told his subjects, for instance, that since they wanted an heir to the throne of distinguished birth he had decided to take a wife of a most illustrious family who had actually been brought up in a convent. The people, of course, did not know that he was speaking of his own daughter. She, too, did not realize that the Prince was actually her father and that it was only his strangely twisted mind which had led him to make this foolish announcement which, even though he had never intended to carry out the plan, would bring so much unhappiness to so many people. He even arranged another match for the young man with whom the princess had fallen so deeply in love.

One can only guess how cruel the news was to the two young lovers. Next, without any sign of concern for her, the Prince told his faithful wife that it was necessary for him to leave her in order to avoid extreme misfortune later on. He explained that his people, shocked by her low birth, were urging him to make a more suitable alliance elsewhere. "You," he said, "will have to go back to your little thatched cottage, after having once more put on the dress of a shepherdess, as I have arranged for you."

Calmly and with a quiet firmness, the Princess listened as he pronounced this sentence on her. Her face serene, she hid her grief and without her sorrow in any way lessening her charms, great tears fell from her eyes. So also, sometimes in April, the rain falls while the sun still is shining.

"You are my husband, my lord and master," she said, sighing, "and whatever else you may hear, you must remember that nothing is nearer my heart than to obey you completely." Therefore she retired alone to her apartments, stripped herself of her expensive wardrobe and, quietly and without a complaint, put on the clothes she had once worn while guarding her sheep.

In her humble carriage she left the Prince with

these words: "I cannot leave you without your pardon for having displeased you. I can bear the load of my own sorrow, but I cannot, my lord, endure your anger. Have pity on my sincere regret and I will live content in my sad abode, knowing that time will never change my humble regard for you or my unbroken love."

Such obedience and nobleness of spirit from one so meanly dressed aroused in the heart of the Prince some remembrance of his early love for her and almost ended the banishment. Moved by her charms and on the verge of tears, he was about to put his arms around her when his domineering vanity suddenly over-came his love. And so he said harshly:

"Of days that are gone I have lost all recollection. I am satisfied with your confession. Come, let us go."

She left immediately and turning to her father who was also dressed once more in his rustic clothes and whose heart was weeping bitterly over this sudden and unexpected change, she said:

"Let us return to our shady groves and our simple life and leave without regret the pomp of this palace. Our cottage is not very elaborate but it does offer more of honesty and rest for us and peace of mind."

When they arrived at their wilderness home, she took up her distaff and spindle and began her spinning on the bank of the same stream where the Prince had first discovered her. A hundred times a day her heart, peaceful and with no bitterness, implored Heaven to bless her husband with fame and riches and to refuse him none of his wishes. A love fed on caresses could not have been warmer than hers.

But her dear husband of whom she was thinking still insisted on testing her further and so he ordered her once again to come and visit him.

"Griselda," he said, when she presented herself, "it is necessary that the princess, to whom I give my hand tomorrow in the church, should understand completely where you and I stand. I therefore insist on your attendance on her and that you help me in every way in pleasing her. You know in what manner I must be served – nothing held back, and nothing too good. Everyone must see in me a Prince – more than that, a Prince in love.

"Use all your energies in preparing her apartment with abundance of everything: richness, neatness and elegance all combined. And finally, always keep in mind that she is a young princess whom I love tenderly. And so that you may carry out your duties completely you must understand that to serve her in every way is my strictest order to you."

As radiant as the morning sun appears in the East, so, too, the lovely princess seemed on her arrival at the palace. At first, in the depths of her heart Griselda felt an ecstasy of mother love when she saw her. Days that were gone, happier days, came back to her in memory. "Alas! my daughter," she said to herself. "If a kind Heaven had heard my prayers, she would be almost as tall and perhaps just as beautiful as this new princess."

For this young princess she felt so deep a love she could not help saying to the Prince: "Permit me to warn you, my lord, that this charming princess who is to be your wife, reared in a life of ease and luxury, will not be able to endure the sort of treatment I have received from you.

"Necessity and my humble station in life have hardened me for work and I can endure all sorts of misfortune without pain and without complaint. But she who has never known grief will die under the least hardship, at the least sharp or unkind word. Do, my lord, I beg you, always treat her with kindness."

"Try to serve me," said the Prince severely, "as well as you can. It is hardly necessary for a simple shepherdess like you to give me lessons or to meddle in my affairs by explaining my duties to me."

At this rebuke, Griselda, lowering her glance, quickly withdrew from his presence.

And now the lords and ladies from far and near began to assemble for the wedding. In a magnificent reception room where they were called together before the ceremony, the Prince addressed them.

"Nothing in the world," he said, "is more deceitful than appearances. Here you can see a shining example. Who among you would not think that this young woman, so soon to be my wife, would be most happy and contented. But she is not at all!

"Who would dare believe that this young man, eager for fame, would not be happy in this marriage we have arranged for him, triumphing over all his rivals? Yet this is not true!

"Again, who would imagine that, with justifiable anger, Griselda would not weep in despair at her lot? Yet she has complained of nothing, has consented to everything I asked of her and nothing whatever has been able to provoke her patience.

"And, finally, who would dream that anything could match my happy outlook for the future in beholding the charms of the object of my vows? If, however, fate should deal unkindly with me in these matters, I shall be most deeply grieved and of all the princes in this world the most unhappy.

"If anything I have said is difficult for you to understand, a word or two further should explain everything – words which should make all the unhappiness of which you may have heard rumours vanish at once.

"Know then," he went on, "that the charming person who has stolen my heart is, in fact, my own daughter and that the woman who is the attendant to the lady, who loves her extremely and is, in turn, loved by her, is really still my beloved wife.

"Know further that, moved by the patience of this wise and faithful wife whom I have driven away and humiliated, I here and now take her back again as far as I can atone for the cruel and harsh treatment she has received from my jealous spirit. It will be my purpose in the future to prevent anything which might bring about this regrettable situation again. And if the memory of these cruel days in which her heart was not once borne down should in after times remain, I hope that even more than this people will speak of the fame with which I have crowned her surpassing virtue."

Just as when a thick cloud has cut off the sun and all the heavens are darkened by a fearful storm, if these clouds are parted by the winds and a brilliant burst of sunlight shines down on the landscape, so that the whole world smiles again and renews its beauty – so in all eyes where sadness had reigned suddenly now a new happiness shone everywhere. For at this announcement, the young princess was enraptured in realizing that she had won back her life again from the Prince. Falling to her knees she embraced him warmly, but her father, who had also won back his beloved daughter, lifted her to her feet, blessed her and led her to her mother.

So much happiness, coming all at once, almost robbed the mother of all feelings. Her great heart which had endured grief so well, almost broke now with the burden of this new joy. Scarcely could she hold in her arms this lovely child of hers whom Heaven had returned to her. All she could do was to weep.

"We have years to come in which to be happy," the Prince told her. "Put on the new wardrobe which your rank demands."

And so together they led the two young lovers to the church where they were married. A thousand diversions followed – tournaments, games, dances, music and great banquets. And everywhere everyone's eyes were on Griselda whose patience under the greatest adversity was praised by all. Indeed, some of the people even praised the Prince's cruelties because they had produced so remarkable a proof of Griselda's constancy that people saw in her a model for women everywhere in the world.

Beauty and the Beast

NCE UPON A TIME there lived a merchant who was exceedingly rich. He had six children – three boys and three girls – and being a sensible man he spared no expense upon their education, but engaged tutors of every kind for them. All his daughters were pretty, but the youngest especially was admired by everybody. When she was small she was known simply as 'the little beauty,' and this name stuck to her, causing a great deal of jealousy on the part of her sisters.

This youngest girl was not only prettier than her sisters, but very much nicer. The two elder girls were very arrogant as a result of their wealth; they pretended to be great ladies, declining to receive the daughters of other merchants, and associating only with people of quality. Every day they went off to balls and theatres, and for walks in the park, with many a gibe at their little sister, who spent much of her time in reading good books.

Now these girls were known to be very rich, and in consequence were sought in marriage by many prominent merchants. The two eldest said they would never marry unless they could find a duke, or at least a count. But Beauty – this, as I have mentioned, was the name by which the youngest was known – very politely thanked all who proposed marriage to her, and said that she was too young at present, and that she wished to keep her father company for several years yet.

Suddenly the merchant lost his fortune, the sole property which remained to him being a small house in the country, a long way from the capital. With tears he broke it to his children that they would have to move to this house, where by working like peasants they might just be able to live.

The two elder girls replied that they did not wish to leave the town, and that they had several admirers who would be only too happy to marry them, notwithstanding their loss of fortune. But the simple maidens were mistaken: their admirers would no longer look at them, now that they were poor. Everybody disliked them on account of their arrogance, and folks declared that they did not deserve pity: in fact, that it was a good thing their pride had had a fall – a turn at minding sheep would teach them how to play the fine lady! "But we are very sorry for Beauty's misfortune," everybody added; "she is such a dear girl, and was always so considerate to poor people: so gentle, and with such charming manners!"

There were even several worthy men who would have married her, despite the fact that she was now penniless; but she told them she could not make up her mind to leave her poor father in his misfortune, and that she intended to go with him to the country, to comfort him and help him to work. Poor Beauty had been very grieved at first over the loss of her fortune, but she said to herself:

"However much I cry, I shall not recover my wealth, so I must try to be happy without it."

When they were established in the country the merchant and his family started working on the land. Beauty used to rise at four o'clock in the morning, and was busy all day looking after the house, and preparing dinner for the family. At first she found it very hard, for she was not accustomed to work like a servant, but at the end of a couple of months she grew stronger, and her health was improved by the work. When she had leisure she read, or played the harpsichord, or sang at her spinning-wheel.

Her two sisters, on the other hand, were bored to death; they did not get up till ten o'clock in the morning, and they idled about all day. Their only diversion was to bemoan the beautiful clothes they used to wear and the company they used to keep. "Look at our little sister," they would say to each other; "her tastes are so low and her mind so stupid that she is quite content with this miserable state of affairs."

The good merchant did not share the opinion of his two daughters, for he knew that Beauty was more fitted to shine in company than her sisters. He was greatly impressed by the girl's good qualities, and especially by her patience – for her sisters, not content with leaving her all the work of the house, never missed an opportunity of insulting her.

They had been living for a year in this seclusion when the merchant received a letter informing him that a ship on which he had some merchandise had just come safely home. The news nearly turned the heads of the two elder girls, for they thought that at last they would be able to quit their dull life in the country. When they saw their father ready to set out they begged him to bring them back dresses, furs, caps, and finery of every kind. Beauty asked for nothing, thinking to herself that all the money which the merchandise might yield would not be enough to satisfy her sisters' demands.

"You have not asked me for anything," said her father.

"As you are so kind as to think of me," she replied, "please bring me a rose, for there are none here."

Beauty had no real craving for a rose, but she was anxious not to seem to disparage the conduct of her sisters. The latter would have declared that she purposely asked for nothing in order to be different from them.

The merchant duly set forth; but when he reached his destination there was a lawsuit over his merchandise, and after much trouble he returned poorer than he had been before. With only thirty miles to go before reaching home, he was already looking forward to the pleasure of seeing his children again, when he found he had to pass through a large wood. Here he lost himself. It was snowing horribly; the wind was so strong that twice he was thrown from his horse, and when night came on he made up his mind he must either die of hunger and cold or be eaten by the wolves that he could hear howling all about him.

Suddenly he saw, at the end of a long avenue of trees, a strong light. It seemed to be some distance away, but he walked towards it, and presently discovered that it came from a large palace, which was all lit up.

The merchant thanked heaven for sending him this help, and hastened to the castle. To his surprise, however, he found no one about in the courtyards. His horse, which had followed him, saw a large stable open and went in; and on finding hay and oats in readiness the poor animal, which was dying of hunger, set to with a will. The merchant tied him up in the stable, and approached the house, where he found not a soul. He entered a large room; here there was a good fire, and a table laden with food, but with a place laid for one only. The rain and snow had soaked him to the skin, so he drew near the fire to dry himself. "I am sure," he remarked to himself, "that the master of this house or his servants will forgive the liberty I am taking; doubtless they will be here soon."

He waited some considerable time; but eleven o'clock struck and still he had seen nobody. Being no longer able to resist his hunger he took a chicken and devoured it in two mouthfuls, trembling. Then he drank several glasses of wine, and becoming bolder ventured out of the room. He went through several magnificently furnished apartments, and finally found a room with a very good bed. It was now past midnight, and as he was very tired he decided to shut the door and go to bed.

It was ten o'clock the next morning when he rose, and he was greatly astonished to find a new suit in place of his own, which had been spoilt. "This palace," he said to himself, "must surely belong to some good fairy, who has taken pity on my plight."

He looked out of the window. The snow had vanished, and his eyes rested instead upon arbours of flowers – a charming spectacle. He went back to the room where he had supped the night before, and found there a little table with a cup of chocolate on it. "I thank you, Madam Fairy," he said aloud, "for being so kind as to think of my breakfast."

Having drunk his chocolate the good man went forth to look for his horse. As he passed under a bower of roses he remembered that Beauty had asked for one, and he plucked a spray from a mass of blooms. The very same moment he heard a terrible noise, and saw a beast coming towards him which was so hideous that he came near to fainting.

"Ungrateful wretch!" said the Beast, in a dreadful voice; "I have saved your life by receiving you into my castle, and in return you steal that which I love better than anything in the world – my roses. You shall pay for this with your life! I give you fifteen minutes to make your peace with Heaven."

The merchant threw himself on his knees and wrung his hands. "Pardon, my lord!" he cried; "one of my daughters had asked for a rose, and I did not dream I should be giving offence by picking one."

"I am not called 'my lord,'" answered the monster, "but 'The Beast.' I have no liking for compliments, but prefer people to say what they think. Do not hope therefore to soften me by flattery. You have daughters, you say; well, I am willing to pardon you if one of your daughters will come, of her own choice, to die in your place. Do not argue with me – go! And swear that if your daughters refuse to die in your place you will come back again in three months."

The good man had no intention of sacrificing one of his daughters to this hideous monster, but he thought that at least he might have the pleasure of kissing them once again. He therefore swore to return, and the Beast told him he could go when he wished. "I do not wish you to go empty-handed," he added; "return to the room where you slept; you will find there a large empty box. Fill it with what you will; I will have it sent home for you."

With these words the Beast withdrew, leaving the merchant to reflect that if he must indeed die, at all events he would have the consolation of providing for his poor children.

He went back to the room where he had slept. He found there a large number of gold pieces, and with these he filled the box the Beast had mentioned. Having closed the latter, he took his horse, which was still in the stable, and set forth from the palace, as melancholy now as he had been joyous when he entered it.

The horse of its own accord took one of the forest roads, and in a few hours the good man reached his own little house. His children crowded round him, but at sight of them, instead of welcoming their caresses, he burst into tears. In his hand was the bunch of roses which he had brought for Beauty, and he gave it to her with these words:

"Take these roses, Beauty; it is dearly that your poor father will have to pay for them."

Thereupon he told his family of the dire adventure which had befallen him. On hearing the tale the two elder girls were in a great commotion, and began to upbraid Beauty for not weeping as they did. "See to what her smugness has brought this young chit," they said; "surely she might strive to find some way out of this trouble, as we do! But oh, dear me, no; her ladyship is so determined to be different that she can speak of her father's death without a tear!"

"It would be quite useless to weep," said Beauty. "Why should I lament my father's death? He is not going to die. Since the monster agrees to accept a daughter instead, I intend to offer myself to appease his fury. It will be a happiness to do so, for in dying I shall have the joy of saving my father, and of proving to him my devotion."

"No, sister," said her three brothers; "you shall not die; we will go in quest of this monster, and will perish under his blows if we cannot kill him."

"Do not entertain any such hopes, my children," said the merchant; "the power of this Beast is so great that I have not the slightest expectation of escaping him. I am touched by the goodness of Beauty's heart, but I will not expose her to death. I am old and have not much longer to live; and I shall merely lose a few years that will be regretted only on account of you, my dear children."

"I can assure you, father," said Beauty, "that you will not go to this palace without me. You cannot prevent me from following you. Although I am young I am not so very deeply in love with life, and

I would rather be devoured by this monster than die of the grief which your loss would cause me." Words were useless. Beauty was quite determined to go to this wonderful palace, and her sisters were not sorry, for they regarded her good qualities with deep jealousy.

The merchant was so taken up with the sorrow of losing his daughter that he forgot all about the box which he had filled with gold. To his astonishment, when he had shut the door of his room and was about to retire for the night, there it was at the side of his bed! He decided not to tell his children that he had become so rich, for his elder daughters would have wanted to go back to town, and he had resolved to die in the country. He did confide his secret to Beauty, however, and the latter told him that during his absence they had entertained some visitors, amongst whom were two admirers of her sisters. She begged her father to let them marry; for she was of such a sweet nature that she loved them, and forgave them with all her heart the evil they had done her.

When Beauty set off with her father the two heartless girls rubbed their eyes with an onion, so as to seem tearful; but her brothers wept in reality, as did also the merchant. Beauty alone did not cry, because she did not want to add to their sorrow.

The horse took the road to the palace, and by evening they espied it, all lit up as before. An empty stable awaited the nag, and when the good merchant and his daughter entered the great hall, they found there a table magnificently laid for two people. The merchant had not the heart to eat, but Beauty, forcing herself to appear calm, sat down and served him. Since the Beast had provided such splendid fare, she thought to herself, he must presumably be anxious to fatten her up before eating her.

When they had finished supper they heard a terrible noise. With tears the merchant bade farewell to his daughter, for he knew it was the Beast. Beauty herself could not help trembling at the awful apparition, but she did her best to compose herself. The Beast asked her if she had come of her own free will, and she timidly answered that such was the case.

"You are indeed kind," said the Beast, "and I am much obliged to you. You, my good man, will depart to-morrow morning, and you must not think of coming back again. Good-bye, Beauty!"

"Good-bye, Beast!" she answered.

Thereupon the monster suddenly disappeared.

"Daughter," said the merchant, embracing Beauty, "I am nearly dead with fright. Let me be the one to stay here!"

"No, father," said Beauty, firmly, "you must go tomorrow morning, and leave me to the mercy of Heaven. Perhaps pity will be taken on me."

They retired to rest, thinking they would not sleep at all during the night, but they were hardly in bed before their eyes were closed in sleep. In her dreams there appeared to Beauty a lady, who said to her:

"Your virtuous character pleases me, Beauty. In thus undertaking to give your life to save your father you have performed an act of goodness which shall not go unrewarded."

When she woke up Beauty related this dream to her father. He was somewhat consoled by it, but could not refrain from loudly giving vent to his grief when the time came to tear himself away from his beloved child.

As soon as he had gone Beauty sat down in the great hall and began to cry. But she had plenty of courage, and after imploring divine protection she determined to grieve no more during the short time she had yet to live.

She was convinced that the Beast would devour her that night, but made up her mind that in the interval she would walk about and have a look at this beautiful castle, the splendour of which she could not but admire.

Imagine her surprise when she came upon a door on which were the words "Beauty's Room"! She quickly opened this door, and was dazzled by the magnificence of the appointments within. "They are evidently anxious that I should not be dull," she murmured, as she caught sight of a large bookcase, a harpsichord, and several volumes of music. A moment later another thought crossed her mind. "If I had only a day to spend here," she reflected, "such provision would surely not have been made for me."

This notion gave her fresh courage. She opened the bookcase, and found a book in which was written, in letters of gold:

"Ask for anything you wish: you are mistress of all here."

"Alas!" she said with a sigh, "my only wish is to see my poor father, and to know what he is doing."

As she said this to herself she glanced at a large mirror. Imagine her astonishment when she perceived her home reflected in it, and saw her father just approaching. Sorrow was written on his face; but when her sisters came to meet him it was impossible not to detect, despite the grimaces with which they tried to simulate grief, the satisfaction they felt at the loss of their sister. In a moment the vision faded away, yet Beauty could not but think that the Beast was very kind, and that she had nothing much to fear from him.

At midday she found the table laid, and during her meal she enjoyed an excellent concert, though the performers were invisible. But in the evening, as she was about to sit down at the table, she heard the noise made by the Beast, and quaked in spite of herself.

"Beauty," said the monster to her, "may I watch you have your supper?"

"You are master here," said the trembling Beauty.

"Not so," replied the Beast; "it is you who are mistress; you have only to tell me to go, if my presence annoys you, and I will go immediately. Tell me, now, do you not consider me very ugly?"

"I do," said Beauty, "since I must speak the truth; but I think you are also very kind."

"It is as you say," said the monster; "and in addition to being ugly, I lack intelligence. As I am well aware, I am a mere beast."

"It is not the way with stupid people," answered Beauty, "to admit a lack of intelligence. Fools never realise it."

"Sup well, Beauty," said the monster, "and try to banish dulness from your home – for all about you is yours, and I should be sorry to think you were not happy."

"You are indeed kind," said Beauty. "With one thing, I must own, I am well pleased, and that is your kind heart. When I think of that you no longer seem to be ugly."

"Oh yes," answered the Beast, "I have a good heart, right enough, but I am a monster."

"There are many men," said Beauty, "who make worse monsters than you, and I prefer you, notwithstanding your looks, to those who under the semblance of men hide false, corrupt, and ungrateful hearts."

The Beast replied that if only he had a grain of wit he would compliment her in the grand style by way of thanks; but that being so stupid he could only say he was much obliged.

Beauty ate with a good appetite, for she now had scarcely any fear of the Beast. But she nearly died of fright when he put this question to her:

"Beauty, will you be my wife?"

For some time she did not answer, fearing lest she might anger the monster by her refusal. She summoned up courage at last to say, rather fearfully, "No, Beast!"

The poor monster gave forth so terrible a sigh that the noise of it went whistling through the whole palace. But to Beauty's speedy relief the Beast sadly took his leave and left the room, turning several times as he did so to look once more at her. Left alone, Beauty was moved by great compassion for this poor Beast.

"What a pity he is so ugly," she said, "for he is so good."

Beauty passed three months in the palace quietly enough. Every evening the Beast paid her a visit, and entertained her at supper by a display of much good sense, if not with what the world calls wit. And every day Beauty was made aware of fresh kindnesses on the part of the monster. Through seeing him often she had become accustomed to his ugliness, and far from dreading the moment of his visit, she frequently looked at her watch to see if it was nine o'clock, the hour when the Beast always appeared.

One thing alone troubled Beauty; every evening, before retiring to bed, the monster asked her if she would be his wife, and seemed overwhelmed with grief when she refused. One day she said to him:

"You distress me, Beast. I wish I could marry you, but I cannot deceive you by allowing you to believe that that can ever be. I will always be your friend – be content with that."

"Needs must," said the Beast. "But let me make the position plain. I know I am very terrible, but I love you very much, and I shall be very happy if you will only remain here. Promise that you will never leave me."

Beauty blushed at these words. She had seen in her mirror that her father was stricken down by the sorrow of having lost her, and she wished very much to see him again. "I would willingly promise to remain with you always," she said to the Beast, "but I have so great a desire to see my father again that I shall die of grief if you refuse me this boon."

"I would rather die myself than cause you grief," said the monster. "I will send you back to your father. You shall stay with him, and your Beast shall die of sorrow at your departure."

"No, no," said Beauty, crying; "I like you too

much to wish to cause your death. I promise you I will return in eight days. You have shown me that my sisters are married, and that my brothers have joined the army. My father is all alone; let me stay with him one week."

"You shall be with him to-morrow morning," said the Beast. "But remember your promise. All you have to do when you want to return is to put your ring on a table when you are going to bed. Good-bye, Beauty!"

As usual, the Beast sighed when he said these last words, and Beauty went to bed quite down-hearted at having grieved him.

When she awoke the next morning she found she was in her father's house. She rang a little bell which stood by the side of her bed, and it was answered by their servant, who gave a great cry at sight of her. The good man came running at the noise, and was overwhelmed with joy at the sight of his dear daughter. Their embraces lasted for more than a quarter of an hour. When their transports had subsided, it occurred to Beauty that she had no clothes to put on; but the servant told her that she had just discovered in the next room a chest full of dresses trimmed with gold and studded with diamonds. Beauty felt grateful to the Beast for this attention, and having selected the simplest of the gowns she bade the servant pack up the others, as she wished to send them as presents to her sisters.

The words were hardly out of her mouth when the chest disappeared. Her father expressed the opinion that the Beast wished her to keep them all for herself, and in a trice dresses and chest were back again where they were before.

When Beauty had dressed she learned that her sisters, with their husbands, had arrived. Both were very unhappy. The eldest had wedded an exceedingly handsome man, but the latter was so taken up with his own looks that he studied them from morning to night, and despised his wife's beauty. The second had married a man with plenty of brains, but he only used them to pay insults to everybody – his wife first and foremost.

The sisters were greatly mortified when they saw Beauty dressed like a princess, and more beautiful than the dawn. Her caresses were ignored, and the jealousy which they could not stifle only grew worse when she told them how happy she was.

Out into the garden went the envious pair, there to vent their spleen to the full. "Why should this chit be happier than we are?" each demanded of the other; "are we not much nicer than she is?"

"Sister," said the elder, "I have an idea. Let us try to persuade her to stay here longer than the eight days. Her stupid Beast will fly into a rage when he finds she has broken her word, and will very likely devour her."

"You are right, sister," said the other; "but we

must make a great fuss of her if we are to make the plan successful."

With this plot decided upon they went upstairs again, and paid such attention to their little sister that Beauty wept for joy. When the eight days had passed the two sisters tore their hair, and showed such grief over her departure that she promised to remain another eight days.

Beauty reproached herself, nevertheless, with the grief she was causing to the poor Beast; moreover, she greatly missed not seeing him. On the tenth night of her stay in her father's house she dreamed that she was in the palace garden, where she saw the Beast lying on the grass nearly dead, and that he upbraided her for her ingratitude. Beauty woke up with a start, and burst into tears.

"I am indeed very wicked," she said, "to cause so much grief to a Beast who has shown me nothing but kindness. Is it his fault that he is so ugly, and has so few wits? He is good, and that makes up for all the rest. Why did I not wish to marry him? I should have been a good deal happier with him than my sisters are with their husbands. It is neither good looks nor brains in a husband that make a woman happy; it is beauty of character, virtue, kindness. All these qualities the Beast has. I admit I have no love for him, but he has my esteem, friendship, and gratitude. At all events I must not make him miserable, or I shall reproach myself all my life."

With these words Beauty rose and placed her ring on the table.

Hardly had she returned to her bed than she was asleep, and when she woke the next morning she saw with joy that she was in the Beast's palace. She dressed in her very best on purpose to please him, and nearly died of impatience all day, waiting for nine o'clock in the evening. But the clock struck in vain: no Beast appeared. Beauty now thought she must have caused his death, and rushed about the palace with loud despairing cries. She looked everywhere, and at last, recalling her dream, dashed into the garden by the canal, where she had seen him in her sleep. There she found the poor Beast lying unconscious, and thought he must be dead. She threw herself on his body, all her horror of his looks forgotten, and feeling his heart still beat, fetched water from the canal and threw it on his face.

The Beast opened his eyes and said to Beauty: "You forgot your promise. The grief I felt at having lost you made me resolve to die of hunger; but I die content since I have the pleasure of seeing you once more."

"Dear Beast, you shall not die," said Beauty; "you shall live and become my husband. Here and now I offer you my hand, and swear that I will marry none but you. Alas, I fancied I felt only friendship for you, but the sorrow I have experienced clearly proves to me that I cannot live without you."

Beauty had scarce uttered these words when the castle became ablaze with lights before her eyes: fireworks, music – all proclaimed a feast. But these splendours were lost on her: she turned to her dear Beast, still trembling for his danger.

Judge of her surprise now! At her feet she saw no longer the Beast, who had disappeared, but a prince, more beautiful than Love himself, who thanked her for having put an end to his enchantment. With good reason were her eyes riveted upon the prince, but she asked him nevertheless where the Beast had gone.

"You see him at your feet," answered the prince. "A wicked fairy condemned me to retain that form until some beautiful girl should consent to marry me, and she forbade me to betray any sign of intelligence. You alone in all the world could show yourself susceptible to the kindness of my character, and in offering you my crown I do but discharge the obligation that I owe you."

In agreeable surprise Beauty offered her hand to the handsome prince, and assisted him to rise. Together they repaired to the castle, and Beauty was overcome with joy to find, assembled in the hall, her father and her entire family. The lady who had appeared to her in her dream had had them transported to the castle.

"Beauty," said this lady (who was a celebrated fairy), "come and receive the reward of your noble choice. You preferred merit to either beauty or wit, and you certainly deserve to find these qualities combined in one person. It is your destiny to become a great queen, but I hope that the pomp of royalty will not destroy your virtues. As for you, ladies," she continued, turning to Beauty's two sisters, "I know your hearts and the malice they harbour. Your doom is to become statues, and under the stone that wraps you round to retain all your feelings. You will stand at the door of your sister's palace, and I can visit no greater punishment upon you than that you shall be witnesses of her happiness. Only when you recognise your faults can you return to your present shape, and I am very much afraid that you will be statues for ever. Pride, ill-temper, greed, and laziness can all be corrected, but nothing short of a miracle will turn a wicked and envious heart."

In a trice, with a tap of her hand, the fairy transported them all to the prince's realm, where his subjects were delighted to see him again. He married Beauty, and they lived together for a long time in happiness the more perfect because it was founded on virtue.